Dear Romance Reader,

Welcome to a world of breathtaking passion and never-ending romance.

Welcome to ***Precious Gem Romances.***

It is our pleasure to present *Precious Gem Romances,* a wonderful new line of romance books by some of America's best-loved authors. Let these thrilling historical and contemporary romances sweep you away to far-off times and places in stories that will dazzle your senses and melt your heart.

Sparkling with joy, laughter, and love, each *Precious Gem Romance* glows with all the passion and excitement you expect from the very best in romance. Offered at a great affordable price, these books are an irresistible value—and an essential addition to your romance collection. Tender love stories you will want to read again and again, *Precious Gem Romances* are books you will treasure forever.

Look for fabulous new *Precious Gem Romances* each month—available only at Wal★Mart.

Kate Duffy
Editorial Director

MOM MEETS DAD

Karen Rose Smith

Nancy, I hope you enjoy it. All my best, Karen Rose Smith

Zebra Books
Kensington Publishing Corp.
http://www.zebrabooks.com

ZEBRA BOOKS are published by

Kensington Publishing Corp.
850 Third Avenue
New York, NY 10022

First Printing: April, 1999
10 9 8 7 6 5 4 3 2 1

Printed in the United States of America

To Anne, my college soul mate—for your friendship through the years.

Love, Karen

One

The bell dinged over the door of the ice cream shoppe as Alex Woodsides entered and waited until his daughter preceded him inside. "Cone, sundae, or banana split?" he asked Kristy as they stepped up to the counter.

"Banana split," she replied with a wide smile, her brown curls bobbing around her face, her green eyes twinkling. She looked like him rather than her mother, and Alex had always thought, at least in that instance, fate had been fair.

The teenager at the counter took their orders. Alex remembered his parents taking him for ice cream after the last day of school. It was a tradition . . . one of those traditions he meant to keep. His father always said, "Tradition makes a man feel secure." At thirty-three, Alex had come to believe his father was right.

A few minutes later Alex sat across from his daughter at one of the round, glass-topped tables. "So tell me what happened to your math grade, honey. Your teacher said you didn't have any problems before the last few weeks. Maybe you and I need to work on it over the summer." His general law practice limited his time with Kristy more than he liked. But if she needed help with schoolwork, they'd find time for that and other activities, too. He'd never regretted accepting sole custody of Kristy from the moment she was born. She was the joy of his life.

Kristy shoved in a spoonful of ice cream. "I was thinking, Dad," she mumbled as she swallowed. "It might be better if Heather's mom helped me. After all, she's a teacher and all. And I really like her. Since she's home for the summer, she has lots of time."

Instantly, Alex pictured Amanda Carson, her shoulder-length, honey-blond hair sweeping along her cheek, her blue eyes sparkling with friendliness whenever they had occasion to speak at parent-teacher meetings or when he dropped Kristy off at Heather's. He knew Amanda was a single parent too, and more than once, he'd thought about asking her out. But ever since Kristy's mother had left them both, he preferred not to tempt fate a second time.

"Don't you think letting Mrs. Carson tutor me would be a good idea?" Kristy prodded.

Alex knew he could help his daughter with math, yet his patience sometimes ran a little thin. A teacher might be able to analyze Kristy's difficulties much faster. "All right. I'll call her when we get home."

Kristy licked whipped cream from her spoon. "Why don't we just stop there on the way?"

He couldn't say no with his daughter looking at him so hopefully. "Sure. Why not?"

As Alex walked up to the door of the compact brick house with its carport, white shutters and pink geraniums planted along the front garden, he compared it to his four-bedroom, two-story Tudor on a two-acre lot only a block away. His gardener maintained a well-kept lawn and trimmed the yews on either side of the front porch into symmetrical roundness. But this little house with its personally cared-for look was charming.

Kristy jabbed the bell and Heather appeared as if by magic. "Hi, Mr. Woodsides. C'mon in. My mom's out back."

He looked at his daughter.

She shrugged. "I told Heather we might stop so you could talk to her mom."

His daughter and Amanda's were together as often as they could manage. They'd probably thought up this idea. He addressed Heather. "Does your mom know we were coming?"

Heather exchanged a look with Kristy, then shook her head, sending her blond ponytail swinging. "Kristy didn't know if you'd go for it."

Her honesty made him smile. "I see. Well, now we'll ask your mom if *she'll* go for it."

Heather led the way through a living room decorated with rose-and-yellow flowered upholstery and lace curtains, into a kitchen with maple-stained cabinets and a table and chairs to match. The small hutch displayed delicate white china. He'd never been inside Amanda Carson's home before. It was charming.

Heather led them out onto the back porch with its old-fashioned wooden swing and pointed down the yard. "She's having problems with the lawn mower. It doesn't want to start. Maybe you can help, Mr. Woodsides." The nine-year-old looked up at him with the same expectant expression Kristy often wore. Just from things Kristy had said, he realized the Carsons were on a tight budget. A lawn mower repair bill was probably an additional expense they didn't need.

"I'll see what I can do," he assured her, rolling up

the sleeves of his shirt in deference to the warm weather. In air-conditioning all day at the office and at home, he'd forgotten how warm June could be.

But then he saw Amanda Carson and realized the temperature suddenly felt a lot warmer. She was standing over the lawn mower, a worried furrow between her brows. Her short cotton blouse tied under her breasts, emphasizing their swell. The skin of her slim waist peeked from between the blouse and her short denim shorts. She'd tied her hair high on her head with some kind of yellow band. This was a different Amanda Carson than he'd seen in the past. She certainly didn't look like a sedate third-grade teacher now!

She looked up when she heard him approach. The smudge of grease on her cheek was as appealing as her long, nicely curved legs. Alex's body stirred, startling him. It had been a very long time since the mere physical appearance of a woman had affected him.

"Mr. Woodsides! Is something wrong?" Amanda blushed prettily as her gaze passed over his navy dress slacks and white shirt.

Suddenly, he wanted to wipe that smudge from her cheek, and just as suddenly, he wanted to touch her skin. "No, nothing's wrong. There's something I'd like to discuss with you. But it looks as if *you* could use some help. Heather said the lawn mower won't start."

Amanda gave the machine a disgusted look. "I thought maybe if I let it sit a while, I could coax it. But this isn't your problem . . ."

A sense of chivalry prodded him. "But if I can fix it, it won't be your problem, either. Let me take a look."

Amanda stepped away from the mower and smiled.

"I won't turn down an offer like that. How about something to drink?"

"Sounds good." Alex forced his attention away from her midriff to the lawn mower. But when she walked to the house, he couldn't keep his gaze from following the sway of her hips. A fantasy popped into his head and he shook it off. He was here for his daughter's sake, and he'd better remember that.

For the life of her, Amanda couldn't figure out why the sight of Alex Woodsides in her yard, tinkering with her lawn mower, should be so disconcerting. She'd probably said twenty words to him since she'd moved to Cedar Grove, Pennsylvania, last summer. Well, maybe fifty.

Opening the refrigerator door, she picked up the iced tea. All right. So he'd appeared unbidden in a dream or two. With his tall, muscled physique, his green eyes, his dark-brown hair, her libido had snatched him out of the world's population to give her a midnight thrill. She remembered one dream in particular . . .

With a sigh, Amanda poured two glasses of iced tea, wondering where the girls had disappeared to. It was steaming hot in Heather's room where they usually hung out. Heather was her best reason for dismissing dreams as well as handsome men in her backyard. Hadn't her marriage and divorce taught her anything?

As she took oatmeal cookies from a canister and arranged them on a plate, she glanced out the window. Good heavens! Alex Woodsides had removed his shirt. All she could do was stare as he pulled on the starter rope. Muscular arms. Broad back and shoulders. Slim waist. And when he turned . . .

She quickly moved to the table with the plate of cookies, but not before she'd glimpsed thick wavy dark hair arrowing down his chest. She'd no sooner carried the glasses to the table when the screen door opened. Suddenly the man from her dreams was standing in her kitchen—hot, sweaty and exceptionally male.

At first she couldn't find her voice. Finally, she managed, "Did you find the problem?"

"Sure did. A gummed-up spark plug." He set it on the counter. "Just take that to the hardware store for a replacement."

She gave a sigh of relief. "Is that all? I thought I'd have to buy a new mower. Thanks."

They stared at each other for a few moments, neither of them moving. Amanda was too aware of Alex's scent, both male and cologne, and the heat that seemed to rise up between them. She had to break the spell and distance herself.

Drawing in a breath, she motioned to the sink. "If you'd like to wash up, Mr. Woodsides . . ."

"Call me Alex," he suggested in a voice that shook her almost as much as the sight of his bare chest.

"Alex," she repeated, feeling dazed.

He smiled. "We might as well be on a first name basis, because I have a proposition to make to you."

His smile was as potent as the rest of him. "A proposition?"

"I'll replace the plug for you and tune up the mower, if you'll agree to tutor Kristy in math. She received a D for the quarter."

"Kristy did?"

"You sound surprised."

"I've overseen their homework a few times when she and Heather were working on it, and she never had a problem. But if she needs help, I'll be glad to work with her."

He turned to the sink and used the soap to wash his hands. Above the running water, he said, "I'll pay you the going rate, of course."

"No."

"No?" He reached for the towel on the counter.

He had such large hands. Long, tapered fingers . . . "I won't take money for helping Kristy."

"Well, do you need anything else fixed?" he asked with a grin that said he wouldn't let her do it for free.

All of a sudden, an inspired idea struck Amanda. He could be the answer to a problem she had to solve. "I have a better idea. You're just the person we need to head a program for Career Day at the elementary school."

Alex's grin vanished. "Why would I fill the bill?"

"Because of your position in the community. You've lived here all your life. I'm sure you have contacts with community businesses. Our committee consists of myself, another teacher, Mrs. Webb, and the school principal."

Alex shook his head. "I don't have that kind of time. As it is I work long days."

His work came first she thought wearily. Shades of her ex-husband. Only he'd had other diversions as well. Alex probably did, too. After all, he was a good-looking bachelor. . . . But she was sure this man had the expertise to make Career Day a success. "This program will benefit Kristy, too."

"Good. But I don't have to be the one to head it up."

"Look, Alex. Parents say they want to become involved in their child's education, but when push comes to shove . . ."

Alex's scowl drew his brows together and the muscles in his shoulders tensed. "Don't try to use guilt on me. It won't work. And if this is what I have to do to get you to tutor my daughter, forget it. I'll do it myself."

"I told you I'll tutor Kristy. You asked how you could repay me."

"You're asking too much."

Amanda kept quiet. She'd won more battles by retreat rather than aggression—not that she wanted to fight with Alex Woodsides.

Sounds in the living room alerted Amanda to the girls' presence. They came into the kitchen with smiles on their faces.

Kristy looked up at Amanda. "Are you going to tutor me?"

She would help Alex's daughter whether he assisted with Career Day or not. "I sure am." Looking at Alex, she asked, "What time is good for you?"

After he gave her a probing look, he responded, "Kristy stays with her grandparents during the day in the summer. So evenings would be best. Or Saturdays."

"I think if we have a good session once a week, I can bring her up to speed," Amanda suggested. "Give it some thought and let me know what's best for you."

Alex draped his arm across his daughter's shoulders. "We should be getting home. I'll give you a call about the time."

As Alex and Kristy went to the door, Amanda followed. She watched Alex pluck his shirt from a low tree limb, then walk with his daughter out of the yard.

Heather tugged on Amanda's arm. "He's cool, isn't he, Mom?"

Cool? Not exactly the word Amanda would use. She gave her daughter a hug. "He seems very . . . nice. Now, why don't you and I take those cookies and iced tea outside and get cooled off? I really think we might have to invest in an air conditioner for my bedroom. On hot nights like this, you could sleep with me."

"You know, Mom, Kristy's house has central air."

Of course, it would. Amanda made a silent vow *not* to think about Alex on hot nights or in his air-conditioned bedroom. She would not think of him at all.

The fire company's week-long carnival was a big event in Cedar Grove. Bingo booths, and stand after stand selling food or chances filled the asphalt parking lot beside the social hall. Rides for small children as well as a large carousel and a Ferris wheel lined the perimeter of the lot at the edge of the street.

Kristy strolled along next to Alex on Saturday evening, sometimes running ahead, sometimes straying to a nearby stand to check out what was going on. "Maybe we'll see Heather and her mom."

Alex had thought about Heather's lovely mother and her request the past two days. In fact, Amanda had invaded his thoughts more than he wanted to admit. "What do you want to be when you grow up?" he asked his daughter, seemingly out of the blue.

Kristy shrugged. "I don't know. A lawyer like you. A teacher like Mrs. Carson. Or maybe . . ." Another shrug. "I don't know, Dad. Why?"

Perhaps Amanda was right. Career Day was something the children needed to broaden their outlook. Even if the project took up his time, he should be more active in educating his daughter. "Mrs. Carson asked me to head up the committee at your school for Career Day in the fall. What do you think?"

"Cool! Then it won't be lame."

Sometimes his daughter's language baffled him, but he knew firsthand she hated being bored.

Just as they rounded a row of stands, he spotted Amanda and Heather at the cotton candy concession. Heather saw them and waved, then pulled her mother their way. "Hey, this is great. Mr. Woodsides, could you ride the Ferris wheel with my mom? She wants to, and I don't. Please?"

"Heather," Amanda protested. "I don't have to ride it."

"Dad loves the Ferris wheel, don't you, Dad?" Kristy chimed in.

The Ferris wheel was not high on his priority list, but he couldn't insult Amanda by refusing to ride with her. Not when she'd graciously decided to tutor his daughter for free. Not when the thought of sitting close to her made his heart beat faster. "I definitely like the Ferris wheel." He held out his arm to Amanda. "I just happen to have a few tickets. Shall we take advantage of the opportunity to see the sights, Amanda?"

Looking uncomfortable, Amanda blushed but took his arm.

Alex tore off two tickets and handed the rest to his daughter. "Ride the carousel, then come back here."

"Can we ride two times?" Kristy asked.

Alex laughed. "Sure. We'll wait for you. Right here. Don't go wandering anywhere else."

As Heather and Kristy ran off, Amanda said, "You don't have to do this, you know."

He looked down into her blue eyes, his gaze drawn to her lips, and realized something as he said it. "I want to."

The Ferris wheel stood only fifty yards away. As they walked toward it, Amanda's hand lying gently on his arm, he irrationally wished they were walking down some tree-lined path far away from crowds. It was crazy. He didn't even *know* this woman, though his body was giving him signals that he would like to know her in more than a casual way.

A bearded older man took their tickets and seated them, latching the safety bar in place. Their seat swung as the wheel turned and stopped to load more passengers. Alex's knee bumped Amanda's, his bare leg rubbing against hers. They both wore shorts and Alex would have been perfectly content to let her leg rest against his, but she moved it away until a few inches separated them from hips to toes.

Resting her hands on the safety bar, she said, "You were right about the spark plug. I replaced it. The mower works fine now."

"*You* replaced it?" Alex asked, unable to hide his surprise.

"The man at the hardware store told me exactly what to do. I might not be a mechanical genius, but I can follow directions."

The Ferris wheel turned again and Alex realized he'd offended her. "I didn't mean to suggest you couldn't. I'm just surprised you even tried."

"Haven't you heard that women of the nineties don't rely on men for their well-being?"

Amanda spoke so softly and so nicely he didn't realize till the last moment that her remark was a slam. "Ouch. Is my traditional background showing?"

Her frown disappeared into a small smile. "Maybe. But so are my insecurities."

"What insecurities? A woman who can manage a classroom full of third graders, raise a daughter, and change her own spark plug shouldn't have any insecurities."

Her blue eyes went all soft and wide. "What a nice thing to say!"

He saw the pulse at her throat beating faster and noticed the white piping on her blue knit top made her skin look creamy and delicate. "I'm not being nice. I'm being honest."

This time when the wheel turned, they ended up at the top. Then, without warning, the ride lurched hard and stopped, their seat swinging hard. Alex instinctively curved his arm around Amanda's shoulders. "Are you all right?"

Her hands gripped the bar. "I think so."

Alex tried to see what was happening on the ground. The man at the control was bent over the gears, examining them. "I don't want to alarm you, Amanda, but we could be stuck up here for a while."

"You *are* kidding." Her face went pale.

"I wish I were. But from the crowd gathering down there . . ."

"The girls. They're going to worry if they think we're in danger."

Even at a moment like this, she was thinking of their

kids. "They'll be able to see us. We'll wave. They'll be okay. Trust me."

The look in Amanda's eyes was a combination of defiance and sadness, giving Alex the impression she didn't trust men much. Had her ex-husband done that to her?

His arm felt right around her and he gave her a gentle squeeze as he had the irrational desire to convince her to trust him. "It will be all right. Talk to me. Tell me about this project you want me to handle."

She tried to look down but when she did, their car tilted and she went very still. "You said it would take up too much of your time."

"I'm reconsidering."

That got her attention. At least for the time being. She looked up at him. "Why?"

"Because I thought about what you said. And I do want to be involved in broadening Kristy's view of the world. So tell me what I'd have to do."

Amanda tried to peer over the side of the seat again, but the swing of their car made her sit still and straight. Composing herself, she gave him a weak smile. "I never thought I'd be pitching you the idea in midair."

"Hey. You've got a captive audience. What more could you want?"

"To be safely on the ground?" she asked rhetorically.

"Pitch, Amanda Carson, and distract us both, or I might come up with something that will do the job in a different way." Kissing her might make them both forget they were hanging thirty feet off the ground.

Her mouth rounded slightly, making kissing her even more tempting. He leaned a little closer.

Amanda sat back against the seat, cleared her throat

and quickly launched into a plan of action for Career Day, including the letters and phone calls that would be necessary, emphasizing the expediency of starting the planning now to get everything accomplished on time.

She was explaining the necessity of meetings to keep everyone on the committee up to date when a siren blared and a rescue van drove into the parking lot.

"Oh, that makes me feel a *lot* better," Amanda muttered under her breath.

With his arm still around her, filled with a protectiveness he'd never experienced for anyone other than his daughter, Alex gently rubbed her arm. "We'll be all right."

"Are you trying to convince me or yourself?" she returned, her blue eyes worried.

"Both of us."

The world seemed to stop. The moment stretched beyond real time. This was closer than he'd been to a woman in years, and the heating of his blood had nothing to do with the danger of being stranded on an amusement ride and everything to do with the woman encircled by his arm. When her lips parted, he wanted to taste them.

But someone shouted up from below, and all at once they were involved in a rescue operation instead of simply being stranded. Within the next half hour, firefighters, ladders, and the fire truck with a mechanical crane and bucket seemed to be everywhere at once.

"They're not going to fix it," Amanda murmured, watching everybody do their job.

"No. They're going to get us off any way they can."

"My gosh, Alex. How are we going to climb out of here with the seat swinging . . ."

Her trembling became a noticeable sign of her fear as she gazed down at the rescue equipment.

"Amanda, look at me," he ordered.

The firm tone of his voice brought her gaze to his. "They know what they're doing. Don't get ahead of yourself. They'll tell us exactly what to do."

His words seemed to register. Finally, she took a deep breath and said, "Calm. We're going to stay calm."

"Yes, we are. Just focus on the fact that you'll be home in your bed sleeping in a few hours."

She closed her eyes and he knew she was imagining exactly that. And he was imagining . . .

Hot thoughts do not help in a crisis, he told himself. But his baser half responded, *No, but they're a great distraction.*

Dusk fell and the brightly colored lights from the concession stands were outshone by emergency beams set up on the ground. Rescue workers tied ropes to Amanda and Alex's seat to hold it steady. The firefighter in the bucket of the mechanical crane held two harnesses in his hands as the device stopped directly in front of their seat.

He was a young man in his mid-twenties with a soothing voice. Handing a harness to Amanda, he said, "First slip that on. Then we'll go from there."

Alex aided Amanda with the many straps of the nylon harness as she slipped it on like a jacket. Her fingers fumbled with the buckles, and he latched them himself, trying to ignore the soft roundness of her breasts, the perfume she wore that was sweetly tempting. It was a bit more awkward and difficult for him to help her with the straps that started at her back waist and had to come through her legs to the front.

Her cheeks became rosy as he caught one of the straps for her.

She mumbled, "I can get it," and avoided his gaze.

As he worked with the second harness, she moved over slightly to give him more room. When he thought of her hands as close to his body as his hands had been to hers, he made sure he didn't need her help.

After they were both secure, with safety lines attached, the firefighter unlatched the safety bar and beckoned to Amanda first. He directed, "Stand up slowly. Then just step over here. They're holding the seat steady from the ground."

She seemed frozen where she was.

Alex took her hand and held it. It was as cold as ice. "Amanda, all you have to do is stand up and take a step. Then you'll be safe. C'mon. Heather and Kristy are waiting for us on the ground. They're watching us right over there." He pointed, and Amanda searched for the girls. She found them. Slowly, she stood. A moment later, she was standing next to the firefighter safely in the metal bucket.

Alex followed her. It was a tight squeeze for the three of them. The only place for his arm was around her waist, his body lodged tight against hers as the bucket lowered. Another firefighter stood on the bed of the truck, ready to help Amanda down the ladder.

Only a few minutes later, they stood on solid ground with their daughters giving them each a huge hug.

"Mom, are you okay?" Heather asked. "You're awful white."

"Hey, Dad. Was it way cool up there?" Kristy asked.

"Honey, it was way high up there," he answered, then took Amanda's arm and led her to a bench sitting alongside a hot dog stand. Flipping a few bills out of his pocket, he said to Heather, "Would you get your mom a soda?"

Amanda protested. "I'm fine. I just feel a little shaky."

Heather took a good look at her mom, then Alex, and said, "I'll get lemonade." Then she scampered off with Kristy at her side, the two of them whispering back and forth.

"I'm fine," Amanda repeated and stood to prove it. Meeting Alex's eyes, she said, "I'm sorry I froze. I'm not usually such a scaredy-cat."

He shook his head. "Amanda Carson, you are anything but a scaredy-cat."

As she gazed at him, impulse and what they'd just experienced together nudged him to curve his arm around her, bend his head, and let his lips graze hers. He was about to do a lot more when Amanda suddenly pushed away.

The expression on her face told him he'd made a monumental mistake.

Two

When Alex's secretary buzzed him, he jabbed the button on the console. "Yes, Georgia?"

"A Mrs. Carson on line two. About Career Day."

Instantly, he pictured Amanda's face after he'd kissed her and felt again the awkwardness of her pushing away. Fortunately or unfortunately, depending on how he wanted to look at it, Kristy and Heather had come running back with Amanda's lemonade. After a fast good-bye, Amanda had quickly shepherded Heather toward their car. Despite attempts to concentrate on everything *but* her, he couldn't get the picture of Amanda on the Ferris wheel with her wide blue eyes, blond hair and beautifully curved lips out of his head.

Because of what had happened, he didn't know if she still wanted his help with Career Day. But apparently the lady didn't get sidetracked from her goal. He pressed the button for line two and picked up the receiver. "Hello, Amanda."

"Good morning, Mr. Woodsides. I . . ."

"After Saturday night, don't you think we can use first names?" Formality and his reaction to Amanda didn't seem to go together.

The few moments of silence on her end told him he'd surprised her. Finally, she said, "I suppose it's not every day I let a man latch me into a rescue harness."

Alex laughed. "Facing a life and death experience changes the rules."

"Even though I acted like it, I don't think the situation was quite that serious. And I do remember you saying you'll consider heading up Career Day."

She obviously didn't want to talk about Saturday night . . . or the kiss. "I did say that," he agreed, wanting to keep a connection to her, realizing he'd decided to work on the program for more reasons than educating his daughter. "Could the committee meet at my house one evening this week? We could get started."

"You've thought about this."

"Some. I'll have my secretary type up an agenda so we'll know exactly where we're going. Would Wednesday night suit you? Seven thirty?"

"That's fine," she said, sounding pleased . . . or maybe just relieved. "I'll call Mrs. Webb and Mr. Davidson," she added. "Thank you for volunteering, Alex. I'll see you Wednesday."

"Wednesday, it is. Good-bye, Amanda."

Alex replaced the receiver, wondering if when he saw her, she'd still pretend his kiss never happened. Even if she pretended, should he?

An interior designer had decorated Alex's house, Amanda thought, as she noted the perfect placement of the landscapes—probably originals—the exact precision of the wallpaper border with its wine and green geometric design, and the coordinated loveseat, sofa and chair that certainly hadn't come from a discount showroom. Everything about Alex Woodsides was Class A quality, and he scared her to death. Or rather the way she felt when she was around him did. That kiss . . .

That kiss had been simply a brushing of lips. Perhaps an overreaction to the situation. Apparently in a crisis, she froze. Alex kissed. It made perfect sense. That's why she hadn't mentioned it and neither had he.

So why was it that as he handed each one of the committee an outline of his ideas, her gaze fell to his lips? And as Mrs. Webb argued with him about how to organize the day, Amanda could only think about how his arm had felt around her, the male scent of him, the heat his hard body generated.

"Don't you think so, Amanda?" Mrs. Webb asked.

The older teacher had caught her not paying attention. Not only did Mrs. Webb not appreciate Amanda's new-fangled interactive teaching strategies, she was constantly critical and condescending. Trying to remember the last thing she'd heard, Amanda bluffed, "I think Alex's ideas are right on the mark."

"Yes, of course they are, dear. But we're discussing how many role models for the children we should bring in," the older woman reminded her.

"I suggested thirty." Alex's green eyes twinkled and Amanda had the strange sensation he'd known *exactly* what she'd been thinking about.

"That would be great if you can get thirty," Amanda agreed quickly.

"You young people think it's easy to move students from one classroom to the other—"

"We can move the speakers," Matt Davidson, the

principal of Cedar Grove Elementary, said diplomatically.

The telephone rang on the other side of the room. When it didn't ring again, Amanda guessed Kristy must have answered it upstairs.

"Dad, it's for you. It's Grandma," Kristy called from the winding wooden staircase near the foyer.

"Got it," he called back and, after excusing himself, strode to the library table beside the double window.

Though she tried to keep her mind on the interchange between Mrs. Webb and Matt, her gaze followed Alex. His conversation lasted a few minutes and he looked disconcerted when he hung up. When he returned to the group, he said, "I think that's all we can cover tonight. Think about the suggestions I made, and we'll get together again in a few weeks. How about Sunday, July second at one o'clock?"

Amanda was beginning to realize Alex was a take-charge kind of man . . . like her ex-husband, who always set up the game and expected everyone to play by his rules. Well, she couldn't buck a volunteer with good ideas, but she could make sure he understood this was a committee, not a dictatorship.

"July second might not be good for everyone," she offered. "You know, with the holiday and all."

Alex looked nonplussed. "Mrs. Webb? Matt? Is there a problem?"

Both of them shook their heads.

With a probing stare, Alex turned his attention to her, and she almost forgot she had a point to make. But then she remembered. "I . . . uh . . . two o'clock would be better for me," she managed, her gaze again finding his lips as if inexorably drawn to them.

"Two it is," Alex agreed. He gestured to the dining

room. "I set up coffee and cookies if you're interested."

"Bake them yourself, Mr. Woodsides?" Mrs. Webb wanted to know.

"Since we'll be working together, please call me Alex," he said to the older teacher with a disarming smile. "My secretary picked up the cookies at the bakery for me. But I did brew the coffee. Help yourselves."

Clara Webb and Matt headed for the dining room. But before Amanda could pass Alex, he caught her arm. "You seem preoccupied tonight."

She'd learned over the past few years it was better to take the offensive rather than be on the defensive. "No more than you after your call. Was that Kristy's grandmother?" The nine-year-old often talked about the good times she had with her grandparents.

Dropping his hand from her arm and rubbing the back of his neck, Alex said, "Dad and Mom received an invitation from friends in Florida. They're leaving at the end of the week. For three weeks."

Immediately Amanda understood. "So you have no one to keep Kristy."

"I'm going to have to call a professional agency, I guess, in Camp Hill. I'll have to interview women tomorrow."

Camp Hill, much larger than Cedar Grove, had everything from shopping malls to professional agencies not found in their small town. "Don't be ridiculous," Amanda found herself saying. "Kristy's welcome to spend her days with Heather. You don't want her staying with a stranger, do you?"

"Of course I don't. But I can't ask you to care for my daughter."

"You're not asking. I'm offering. Maybe I just feel

guilty because Heather always wanted a sister and she's found that kind of relationship with Kristy. She's really no bother, Alex. And I can begin tutoring sessions."

"I'll pay you," he said firmly after thinking about it for a few moments.

"You will not!"

He scowled and studied her. When she didn't back down, the scowl disappeared, though his expression was still serious. "If you won't accept payment, you have to promise me something."

Her heart beat fast and she wondered how much promises meant to Alex because they meant a whole lot to her. "What?"

"If you ever need legal counsel, you'll come to me. No charge."

That was an easy promise to keep. She extended her hand. "It's a deal."

When Alex clasped her fingers, tingles danced up her arm. She felt calluses, signifying the fact he didn't spend all of his time behind a desk. Liking the feel of his skin against hers just a little too much, remembering his lips on hers, she pulled away.

Footsteps on the staircase enabled her to turn her attention away from Alex.

"Meeting over?" Heather asked as she came up beside her mother.

"What did Grandma want?" Kristy asked, before Amanda could answer.

Alex smiled at both girls. "The meeting is over, and Grandma and Granddad are going to Florida. But Amanda said you can stay with Heather during the day if you'd like until they get back."

"Cool! When are they leaving?" Kristy asked with a

grin that stretched from one side of her face to the other.

"Friday morning. Is that all right, Amanda? About eight thirty?"

"Eight thirty is fine. And Kristy, bring your bathing suit. We'll go swimming in the afternoon."

Kristy looked up at Alex. "I'm gonna like this, Dad."

As Alex's gaze settled back on Amanda, thanking her, unsettling her, she decided she'd take Kristy under her wing, but her father was an entirely different matter. She'd keep her distance no matter how close their daughters became.

Suppertime came and went on Friday with Amanda checking the clock every fifteen minutes. Alex still hadn't arrived to pick up Kristy and it was after seven thirty! Because Alex's presence put her in a tailspin, no matter how much she'd like to deny it, she'd forgotten to ask him what time he usually finished his work day. But as the time had slipped by and Alex hadn't arrived, she'd made hamburgers on the grill. Thoughtlessness had been one of her ex-husband's major flaws along with his need to control. It looked as if Alex might belong in the same category.

She wasn't disappointed, she told herself, as she squeezed lemons to make a pitcher of lemonade.

She was plucking the seeds from the lemon juice when a sharp rap at the back door startled her. A second later, Alex stood in her kitchen.

"Sorry I'm late," he said with a crooked smile that she guessed was supposed to make up for his lack of consideration.

"And just how late are you?"

The tone of her voice made him frown. "I had an appointment with a couple working out a divorce settlement. It got complicated."

"Too complicated for you to call?"

"As a matter of fact, it was. I didn't want them going for each other's throats. And if I had left, I was afraid my client's husband's attorney would take advantage of my absence. Is there a problem?"

"Yes. You didn't tell me you'd be this late."

He looked around the kitchen, then at her attire—an old pair of shorts and a much washed top, and asked, "You had plans?"

"That's not the point. Did you ever think Kristy might be worried?"

"She knows I work late hours sometimes. She's used to it. I hope you didn't put irrational fears in her head."

"Of course, I didn't. But from here on, if you want Kristy to stay here, I expect a phone call if you're going to be late."

"Maybe you should reconsider your offer," he replied, his jaw tense, his attitude suggesting no one was going to tell him what to do.

How had she gotten mixed up in this anyway? Because she'd wanted to be nice? Her niceness had encouraged her to believe her husband when he'd said he was going away on business, and it had also led her to accept his long work hours and minimal attempts at intimacy. "Nice" meant not rocking the boat. It meant not arguing. It meant being taken advantage of.

"Maybe I should reconsider." Wiping her hand on a towel, she said, "I'll tell Kristy you're here."

As she went through the doorway to the living room,

she realized Kristy and Heather were sitting on the floor, playing a game they'd set up on the coffee table. She hoped they hadn't heard the exchange in the kitchen. It would be up to Alex to decide where his daughter would stay.

"They were mad," Kristy said into the phone in a hushed voice on Saturday morning, worrying that her plan and Heather's to become *real* sisters might have gotten derailed. "I think Dad's looking for somewhere else for me to go." But she didn't want to stay anywhere else, and she wanted to see her dad and Mrs. Carson looking at each other like they had the night they were stuck on the Ferris wheel.

"Mom hasn't said anything," Heather responded to her friend's anxious tone. "All we have to do is get them in the same place again. They like each other. I can tell. And I've told her how your dad takes you horseback riding and skating, and he's home every night. My dad was never around. Sometimes, he didn't even remember my birthday! Mom sent me a Christmas card last year with his name on it. She thinks I couldn't tell. But I could. I'd love having your father for a real dad."

"And I'd love to have your mom for a real mom. I've never had one." She and Heather had talked often about being sisters and having two parents. With determination, Kristy added, "Your mom knows I want to be with you. Just tell her that again. And I'll tell Dad again what a great time I had with you and your mom."

"Can you come over today?" Heather asked.

"Nope. We're going over to Grandma's to check

the house and water the plants, then Dad said something about driving to the mountains. But tomorrow I can get him to take me swimming. How about you?"

"No problem."

"Just look for the orange towel. If it rains, I'll call you and we'll think of something else. We'll fix it. We'll get them liking each other again."

Half of the population of Cedar Grove seemed to gather at the community pool on hot Sunday afternoons. Amanda and Heather emerged from the women's dressing area, their duffel bags in hand, and looked for a spot to sunbathe.

Heather pointed to a narrow area of grass next to an orange towel. "Over there, Mom." After she ran ahead, she plopped down her bag and spread out her towel.

Amanda threaded her way across the grass with more care than Heather. Dropping her duffel bag, she flicked open her towel to lay edge to edge with her daughter's.

Settling on the terrycloth, she found her lotion in her bag and poured some into her hand. When she noticed Heather doing the same, she rubbed it onto her legs.

"Uh . . . Mom?"

Amanda looked over at her daughter and saw the man standing behind her. The one person she hadn't expected to see. The one person she didn't want to see. Especially the way he was dressed. Rather, wasn't dressed. His red swim trunks left nothing to her imagination. And all that tan skin . . .

"Hello, Amanda."

She nodded, "Alex," then decided more explanation was in order. "I didn't know that was your towel."

"I guess you didn't," he replied.

The drops of water nestled in his chest hair glistened in the sun. She couldn't help but be fascinated by it, by his flat stomach, by . . .

"Mom, we're gonna swim. See you in a bit," her daughter informed her as she jumped up.

"Be careful," Amanda warned. Even though the lifeguard kept a close watch, she usually kept an eye on her daughter herself.

"You, too, Kristy," Alex called as the girls hurried to the pool.

Left alone with Alex, Amanda focused her attention on applying lotion to her arms. Peeking at him, she watched as he sat on his towel and took a magazine from his carry-all. He seemed oblivious to her presence. She could pretend he wasn't there just as well.

But when she fished in her bag for a mystery novel she'd tucked in, she knew he was watching her. When she raised her head, their eyes met. Alex didn't look away.

The sun beat down on Amanda's head, but that heat she didn't seem to mind. Aware of the cleavage her black swimsuit showed, the French cut legs, and the way Alex's eyes slowly traveled over her, she could only manage one coherent thought and spoke it aloud. "I'm going to cool off with the girls."

A raised eyebrow was his only response.

Summoning up every shred of composure inside her, she stood and walked to the pool, sensing Alex watched every ripple of her fanny as she moved. Damn the man for making her feel so self-conscious.

Once in the water, she relaxed. It was cold but felt

great on her hot skin. She found an open stretch of water and dove underneath, coming back up to swim a few strokes. After swimming back and forth a few times, she looked around for the girls. To her dismay, she spotted Alex playing pitch and catch with them with a small sponge ball. Just dandy!

Heather and Kristy motioned to her to join in the game. She couldn't refuse without a good reason and she didn't have one. She couldn't tell Kristy, "I don't want to be around your dad because he makes my skin tingle," nor could she admit to her own daughter that in some ways, Alex Woodsides reminded her of Heather's father. Not that her ex-husband had ever shown the kind of caring for Heather that Alex obviously felt for Kristy.

Wading over to her daughter, she plastered on a smile. Before she'd stopped, Kristy tossed the ball. "Catch, Mrs. Carson!"

Instinctively, Amanda raised her hands, and the ball smacked into her palm.

"Good catch, Mom. Let's get it going really fast."

After a feigned toss to Kristy, Amanda instead threw it hard at Alex. But he must have expected her ploy because he was on guard and had no problem catching it. The swiftness with which he pitched it back threw her off balance, but she managed to catch it and pass it to her daughter.

The tosses came faster, the ball hit the water harder, and Amanda had to dive for Kristy's last throw. But apparently Alex thought his daughter had aimed at him because he went after the ball at the same time. Amanda first felt the impact of a hard shoulder against hers. Coming to the surface quickly for a breath, she bumped into Alex's chest as she tried to tread water.

His extra six inches of height allowed him the freedom of standing on the bottom of the sloping pool.

Obviously thinking he was helping, he held her by the waist and lifted her into more shallow water. "Did I hurt you?" he asked, concern evident in his green eyes. Today she noticed amber flecks in them, making them more intense, more mesmerizing.

"I'm fine." His hands, still on her waist, burned through the thin fabric of her suit. Water dripped down her face from her hair and she wanted to wipe it away, but somehow in their collision her hands had ended up clasping his forearms.

Alex's wet hair fell over his brow, the sun glimmered on the reddish highlights, and the nerve along his jaw worked. Then two teenage boys splashed beside them, and Alex released his hands from her waist and brushed his hair back.

Waving to Kristy and Heather, he called, "We're getting out for a while." Then he found the ball floating beside him in the water and tossed it to Kristy.

Unsettled though she was, Amanda still had the presence of mind to realize he was making a decision for her. "Maybe I'm not ready to get out."

"I'd like to talk to you, Amanda."

It wasn't a demand but a very firm request that meant if they didn't talk now, they would eventually. "All right," she acquiesced, deciding it was the only reasonable, adult tactic to take.

She let Alex lead the way so she could get a good view of *his* backside. But as he glanced over his shoulder, and his lips twitched, she had the distinct feeling he'd guessed her motive. And when she watched him stride ahead of her . . .

Blushing was becoming a new hobby.

At her towel, she reached into her bag for a smaller version and dried her hair. When she finished, Alex's gaze was on her. "What?" she asked.

He shrugged. "You did that so unself-consciously. As if I weren't here. Most women I know wouldn't get their hair wet in the first place and if they did, they'd hide in the ladies' room until it was in place again."

She laughed and combed her fingers through her hair to get it away from her face. "I'd be in the ladies' room all the time instead of swimming! Believe me, teaching third graders puts it all in perspective, as well as having a daughter of my own and just wanting to have a little fun."

"Were you? Having fun?" he asked, dropping his towel on the grass.

"Didn't I look like it?"

"Not at the beginning."

She thought back to their disagreement.

"Look, Amanda. I've been thinking about what happened."

He came closer. Close enough to touch. She waited.

Alex's frown made the lines around his eyes deeper. "My parents and Kristy are used to my working irregular hours. When you said you'd watch Kristy, I really didn't think about how my day would affect you. I'm sorry if you worried. I apologize if I took advantage of you."

"Then you'd still like me to watch Kristy?" she asked, wondering if his apology was simply the expedient thing to do.

"That's not the reason I apologized," he said with an edge of anger, then stepped away from her toward his towel.

Jeff had made her suspicious of pretended sincerity,

but she shouldn't transfer her feelings about her ex-husband to Alex. Biting her lip, she clasped his elbow. "I'm the one who's sorry. Can we start with a clean slate?"

As Alex towered over her, she stood perfectly still. He glanced at her hand and she let go. "A clean slate sounds good." He smiled, and Amanda's heart skipped a few beats.

She smiled back.

In the pool, Heather nudged Kristy. And they smiled, too.

Rain, rain and more rain. Amanda had never seen so much. Not only did she have scattered puddles in the basement, but Kristy and Heather were restless after being cooped up for two days. So she decided to take them shopping on Wednesday in Camp Hill about twenty miles away. She'd told Alex her intentions when he dropped off Kristy that morning. He'd had no objections.

Alex Woodsides was taking over entirely too many of her thoughts. After their truce at the pool, he'd told her a little about his law practice, and she'd related a few anecdotes about her years teaching, all the while too aware of his muscular physique and the sexual tension zipping between them. She didn't need a man in her life. She didn't need complications, she reminded herself again and again. But when she stared into those green eyes and he tilted his head and really listened to her—

His full attention was even more seductive than the

idea of his kiss. Not that she was thinking about that, either!

So . . . she decided the shopping excursion was a good idea for all of them.

As Amanda led Heather and Kristy into Camp Hill's largest department store, they asked if they could try out the perfumes on the glass counter. Amanda agreed and all three of them ended up smelling a little too fragrant. But what could make a woman feel more feminine or a young lady more grown-up than perfume?

Except maybe lingerie. Amanda was tagging along behind Kristy and Heather through the department when she spied a beautiful ice-blue teddy hanging on a mannequin. She couldn't help but stop and think . . .

"It matches your eyes, Mrs. Carson. You oughta buy it," Kristy said when she glanced over her shoulder and saw her eyeing it.

"Yeah, Mom. It looks like it would fit."

Amanda lifted the price tag and grimaced. After a wistful sigh, she smiled. "Let's go look at the new fashions for fall." Although it was still June, Amanda would start building Heather's wardrobe with sale items.

At only age nine, Kristy and Heather still knew exactly what they liked. "Does your dad take you shopping for clothes?" Amanda asked Kristy.

Kristy bobbed her head. "With Grandma. We do it two times a year. All at once. He says that's *efficient.*"

Amanda laughed.

"But I like to look and look and look and he just wants to buy, so it's great coming here with you. I don't know what he'll do when I have to get a bra. Let Grandma help me, I guess. He gets so funny about that kind of stuff."

"I imagine it's hard for him to think about you becoming a pretty young lady and growing up."

"I guess. Sometimes, I just really miss having a mom. Dad and Grandma and Granddad are great, but. . . . It's not the same."

Her heart went out to the nine-year-old. Amanda had never really known her own father. And when her mother had died during her sophomore year at college, she'd never experienced such devastation. She'd married Jeff to have a family again. Only it hadn't worked out. Fortunately, she *did* have Heather.

Draping her arm across Kristy's shoulders, she said, "Maybe when it comes time to buy a bra, you and Heather and I can shop."

Kristy gave Amanda a surprise hug. "That'd be great, Mrs. Carson."

Amanda glanced at Heather to see how she was reacting to Kristy's gesture. But she was smiling, and Amanda suddenly felt as if she'd gained a daughter.

Midafternoon, Alex was sitting in a meeting with a client when his secretary informed him his daughter was on the phone.

Afraid Amanda and the girls had been in an accident on the wet roads or something just as serious, he took the call.

"What's wrong, honey?" His heart pounded.

"Mrs. Carson's basement is flooded. She checked it when we got home and *everything* is all wet. She has to try and move all the boxes and doesn't have anywhere to put them. She needs help, Dad."

Alex checked his watch and glanced at his client. "Give me a half hour and I'll be there."

"Great!"

Alex hung up, picturing Amanda standing in a foot of water.

Exactly a half hour later, he parked his car at the curb and ran to the front door. The rain had let up, but the drizzle was enough to dampen his hair and shirt. No one answered the bell, and the door stood open, so he walked in. In the kitchen he heard sounds from the basement. That door stood open, too.

As he descended the steps, he realized he heard chatter and laughter. And when he reached the bottom step, he saw his daughter splashing water at Heather and Amanda with a huge rag mop! All three of them wore flip-flops and water came above their ankles. Open cartons stood everywhere. Apparently Amanda was emptying the wet boxes and the girls were playing at mopping up the mess.

Some disaster!

Amanda spotted him before the girls did. "What are you doing here?" She set aside a photograph album on top of the hot water heater.

"Hey, Dad. Just in time to help." Kristy tugged on Heather's arm and added, "Let's go to the garage to get more dry boxes for your mom."

In a flash the two girls had brushed by him and scampered up the steps.

Amanda came over to him and stood on the bottom step beside him, out of the water.

"Kristy called me." He couldn't seem to keep his gaze away from Amanda's water-spotted cotton blouse and the outline of her lacy bra. "She said you needed help."

Consternation passed over Amanda's face. "I had no idea she called. Everything's fine. Really."

He motioned to the water-filled basement and water-logged boxes. "It doesn't look fine. You need a sump pump. Did you know the basement took in this much water when you bought the house?"

Amanda's shoulders squared, and her blue eyes became a deeper blue. "No, I did not know. The disclosure statement stated 'occasional puddles,' and I'd like to believe that's true. I'll get this mess cleaned up, and wait till it dries out. Then I'll put my stored items on orange crates or something . . ."

The bid for independence in her stance, the damp tendrils of her blond hair curling along her cheek, her blouse plastered against her breasts sent a surge of desire through Alex and he knew only one way to appease it.

He kissed her.

Three

Amanda's breath caught in her chest as she came up against Alex. All of him. His lips were hot, his arms were strong, and his kiss stirred up feelings, and sensations, and excitement that she hadn't felt in years—maybe never. His tongue breached her lips, and before she could protest about the invasion, she got caught up in that, too. His taste bore the richness of coffee, and his scent was male mixed with spice. The heat of his body against hers created a sexual steaminess that surrounded them. Her hands slid into his hair, and as he changed the angle of his mouth on hers, the need to be joined to him shook her. As her breasts pushed against his chest, he groaned.

The sound was sensually stirring because he wanted her. How long had it been since a man had wanted her? How long had it been since she wanted a man? Sex had become a memory from her marriage, and not always an altogether pleasant one. But sex with Alex . . .

Sex? She was thinking about sex? With a man she hardly knew? What was happening to her?

As soon as the thoughts became louder than pleasure, she yanked away from him.

"Whoa," he said, catching her before she fell from the bottom step. His voice was husky, his eyes hazy with lingering desire. And she knew she'd stopped just in time—before he got the wrong idea about her . . . about the whole situation.

"The girls will be back any minute," she murmured.

"That's why you pulled away?"

She couldn't lie to him. "Not exactly."

"Then why exactly?" he asked, his lawyer's determination to find out what he wanted to know evident in his tone.

She couldn't tell him she was afraid of his kiss. She couldn't tell him she hadn't kissed a man since her husband. So . . . in order to cover her insecurity, she said, "It was just a kiss, Alex. It just happened. Now I have to get back to cleaning up my cellar."

His stance became rigid, his expression guarded. "I see. Well, I guess Kristy was wrong. You don't need my help."

"I appreciate you stopping by, Alex, but really, I have everything under control." Though she certainly didn't feel like it, with her knees still shaking and her hands trembling. She clutched them behind her back so he couldn't tell she was affected so strongly by him, let alone the touch of his lips on hers—and everything else that went with it.

"Fine," he said, his jaw set as he mounted the stairs. Halfway up he looked over his shoulder. "I'll be on time to pick up Kristy tonight, Amanda."

Summoning up every ounce of her composure, Amanda nodded. "She'll be ready."

After a last long probing appraisal that made her feel naked as well as vulnerable, he climbed the stairs and disappeared from her sight.

Amanda sagged against the wall. Alex Woodsides

made her feel alive, confused and altogether too . . . hot.

As she brushed her hair from her forehead, she took a deep cleansing breath and let it out slowly. She could get this mess cleaned up by supper time. After all, she had everything under control.

Pulling out the deli containers from the refrigerator, Alex set them on the table at noontime on Saturday as Kristy and Heather ran into the screened-in porch and burst into the kitchen. The girls peeked into each container Alex had opened. "You have all my favorite things," Heather said, looking up at him.

"That's because they're my favorite things, too," Kristy responded with a smile. "I'm glad your mom said you could stay for lunch."

"She's gonna be busy this afternoon. I think she's going to get her hair trimmed."

Alex wondered why Amanda was getting her hair cut. It didn't need it. Everything about her was perfect. Except . . . she'd given him the impression their second kiss had been no big deal. He had to admit, it had been a big deal to him. He'd wanted to take her then and there. He'd wanted to fly her to some remote island so they could be alone for a month. He'd wanted to . . . Damn! He'd wanted to satisfy a physical need and he might as well admit it. That was all.

But he was still curious about Amanda and why she was getting her hair trimmed. Perhaps she was going out tonight. He didn't like pumping Heather for information, but a little investigating wouldn't hurt. "Is your mom going someplace special?" Alex asked.

Heather hesitated only a few moments, then after

a quick look at Kristy, she answered, "Uh . . . mom goes someplace special almost every weekend."

"I see."

Amanda's daughter went on, "She likes to get dressed up and wear perfume and lipstick and do her hair."

Now he was sorry he'd asked. Amanda's nonchalance after their kiss told him she probably got a lot of attention from men. Hell, she probably went out with a different one every weekend. But he wasn't going to get into that with her daughter. Instead, he tore open a bag of potato chips and pushed them to the girls' side of the table.

Suddenly he wasn't the least bit hungry.

Kristy ran ahead of Heather, past the lean-to her dad had built, through the fringe of woods to the edge of the creek.

When Heather caught up to her, she said, "Your dad told us to stay away from the creek."

Glancing at her friend, Kristy grinned. "Dad worries too much. This old tree is a great bridge. You aren't afraid when we cross it, are you?"

"A little." Heather brushed her ponytail from her shoulder. "But it's worth it to look down from up there." With a smile she pointed to the giant oak on the other side of the creek.

Kristy hopped up onto the tree. Putting one foot in front of the other on the weather-beaten fallen trunk connecting the two banks of the creek, she stretched out her arms for balance.

Heather stepped up behind Kristy, keeping her gaze on the log. "Your dad was quiet at lunch."

"Maybe he's thinking about asking your mom out."

"Think he will?" Heather asked, afraid she was going to lose her balance, but proceeding anyway.

"Well, you told him she likes to get dressed up. That was good." Kristy hopped up onto the bank and waited for Heather at the base of the oak.

"And I didn't lie when I said she goes someplace special every weekend. She *does*. She goes to church!" Heather said as she reached the bank.

"But he thought you meant out on dates."

Heather shrugged as if to say she couldn't help what Alex thought.

Kristy pushed her brown curls out of her eyes and said, "Let's climb."

As usual, Kristy went up the oak first, jumping up to catch hold of the lowest branch, then shimmying her way to the trunk. She waited while Heather did the same. When she'd first met Heather, her new friend had been quiet, reading books more than she played outside. But as spring had come, Kristy had convinced Heather to play with her in the lean-to at the edge of the woods bordering her house. She'd also taught her how to climb a tree.

They settled on their favorite branches, Kristy only about a foot above Heather. "I think we should tell your mom my dad's going out tonight," Kristy said.

Heather swung her legs back and forth. "Why?"

"So then she'll think it's really special when he asks her out."

"If he asks her out."

"He will. And he is going out tonight, you know."

Heather looked puzzled. "He is?"

"Yep, to the grocery store."

Both girls swung their legs and laughed, sure their plan was going to work.

Checking the final problem on Kristy's work sheet for accuracy Monday afternoon, Amanda was puzzled. Her student sat across from her finishing another set of math problems, but she didn't seem to be having any trouble doing them and every problem on the sheet in front of Amanda was correct. When the telephone rang, Amanda pushed her chair back and crossed to the counter, lifting the receiver from the wall phone.

"Amanda, it's Alex."

He didn't need to identify himself. She knew his voice. She also wondered where he'd gone on a date on Saturday night and, more important, who he'd taken. Kristy had told her that her dad was going out. Amanda shouldn't have been surprised. A man like Alex had to be in demand. He probably had women lined up who couldn't wait to be seen on his arm. That thought had kept her coolly polite to Alex when he'd dropped Kristy off this morning. He'd been just as polite. She couldn't think about him or look at him without remembering that kiss.

But she kept her voice even and calm, despite her racing pulse. "Hello, Alex. Do you need to talk to Kristy?"

"No. I just wanted to warn you that I'll be a little late."

"A little?" she asked.

After a few moments of silence, she heard his sigh. "The truth is, Amanda, I have an appointment at five and I don't know how long it will go. Is that a problem?"

There was no reason she should make this difficult for Alex. She certainly didn't have any plans, and she enjoyed spending time with the girls as much as they enjoyed spending time with each other. Her voice softened. "No, it's not a problem. I'll find something that will keep them out of trouble," she teased.

After a pause, he responded, "We're lucky, aren't we?"

She knew exactly what he meant. Both girls were a joy to raise. "We are," she agreed.

He suggested, "I could stop for ice cream on my way."

Sometimes she felt as if he thought he owed her for taking care of Kristy. "Alex, I know you probably just want to get home. You don't have to."

"Don't you like ice cream?" he asked with amusement.

She laughed. "Of course I do. Probably more than the girls—especially peanut butter ripple."

"I can take a hint," he assured her.

Thinking about some unknown beauty on his arm, she tried to find the cool politeness she'd used that morning. But somehow in the midst of this conversation, she'd lost it. "Alex, don't worry about your appointment running long. I understand."

There was a long, awkward silence until finally he spoke again. "Are you dating anyone regularly?"

That was an odd thing for him to ask, considering she wasn't dating anyone. She could be coy, she could play hard-to-get, and she could hide in her house and keep herself safe. But suddenly she didn't want to do any of those. "No, I'm not dating anyone regularly." Then she waited for him to ask her out.

But he didn't—he didn't even comment. He just said, "I'll be there as soon as I can. Thanks, Amanda." And he hung up.

Amanda thought about their conversation all afternoon and it still didn't make sense. She'd been presumptuous to think Alex would ask her out, but if he didn't intend to, why had he asked if she was dating somebody regularly? Unless he was worried about her morals and how they'd affect his daughter. That thought made her a bit indignant.

By the time the afternoon had passed and she'd made tacos for supper, she wasn't sure how she'd act around Alex when he arrived. In the meantime, she asked the girls if they'd like to make some chocolate chip cookies. Nothing went better with peanut butter ripple ice cream.

Kristy and Heather were helping to shovel the last cookies off the tray onto the cooling rack when Alex appeared at the back door. His sharp rap brought Amanda's attention to him, and she wondered why the man always had such an impact on her. It had nothing to do with his rolled-up dress shirtsleeves, his tugged-down tie or even the slip of a smile as he held up the bag with the ice cream. Maybe it was because he was so tall or his shoulders so broad. Maybe it was because of just who he was, the whole package—male with a sense of determination and a strength she wished she could bottle, not to mention the sex appeal that just oozed from him. *Why should any of that have an impact?* she thought wryly.

Heather called, "Come on in, Mr. Woodsides."

Kristy looked at the shape of the bag and guessed, "Ice cream, Dad?"

He nodded. "Mrs. Carson's favorite, I'm told." As he set the package on the table, he said, "Something smells terrific."

When his gaze shifted to Amanda, it occurred to her that her pink-and-white knit top and pink shorts were a little skimpy. But she'd dressed to bake cookies, and without air conditioning . . . She shouldn't care what she looked like, she thought, as she brushed her hair behind one ear, her cheeks suddenly hotter than they'd been a few moments before.

An impulse, or an attempt to get his attention off of her, led her to pick up a cool cookie and hold it out to him. "Want to taste test?"

His eyes immediately burned with a light that excited her. "Sure do," he responded, his voice deep and husky, reminding her again of their kiss.

Certain she was reading something into his words that wasn't there, she picked up the canister on the counter and started storing the cooled cookies.

"These are even better than my mother's," he remarked.

"And Grandma makes great cookies," Kristy added.

Amanda bumped his daughter's shoulder and said in an aside, "I think he just wants us to stack up a few more to have with that ice cream."

Giggling, Kristy nodded her agreement as she and Heather went to another cupboard and pulled out dishes.

"We can go out on the porch," Amanda suggested. "It's cooler out there."

Barely ten minutes later, Alex and Amanda sat alone on the old-fashioned wooden porch swing, a good six inches between them. It hadn't taken long for Kristy and Heather to finish cookies and ice cream and head for the jungle gym. Amanda suddenly wished she could go play with them. Sitting on the swing alone with Alex was tough on the nervous system.

"Kristy's doing well with the work you're giving her," Alex commented. "I've been going over the work sheets and she's hardly making any mistakes."

"I know." Still puzzled as to why Kristy had had trouble in the first place, Amanda asked, "Do you mind if I call her teacher?"

"No. I don't mind. Is there a problem?"

"I'd just like to find out exactly when she started falling back. She's an intelligent girl, Alex, and a hard worker. I'm not sure why she started having difficulty, and I'd like to find out when her teacher noticed it first happening."

"It could be that math just baffles her now and then. But if you feel calling her teacher will help, go ahead."

Amanda set her empty ice cream dish on the concrete beside her and decided she would.

Out of the blue, Alex asked, "Do you like to dance?"

It took her a while to shift gears. "Dance?"

His smile was crooked. "Yeah, you know—waltz, tango, stand on the floor and wave your arms around making a fool out of yourself."

She laughed. "Waltz, maybe. I've never tangoed, and as far as making a fool of myself anywhere, I try to avoid that as much as possible."

His expression became more serious. "My high school reunion is on Saturday. They're having it in the reception hall at the Bridgeton Center. I was going to go alone, but it would definitely be more fun if I had a dance partner. Would you like to go with me?"

The Bridgeton Center catered weddings and parties of all types. It was elegant, and Amanda knew she would have to spend money on a new dress if she said yes. So much for buying an air conditioner. But it had been a very long time since a man had asked her out. She and Jeff had met at a fraternity party, and she hadn't dated much up until that point. He'd been attentive and serious about her almost right from the start. She hadn't realized his controlling tendency could smother her and make her feel as though she couldn't make a correct decision until a year into their marriage when she was already pregnant.

She'd been raised to believe in marriage and to give it every chance, and with a baby on the way, she'd wanted to. But Jeff's constant criticism, his taste for giving orders, and finally his infidelity, had severed any bonds they had once forged. She was still wary of getting involved with anyone, but then Alex wasn't asking her to get involved. He was only asking her to accompany him to his high school reunion.

When she didn't respond right away, he frowned. "If you already have plans . . ."

Quickly she shook her head. "No. No, I don't. I think that sounds like fun."

He looked relieved, and she wondered why he hadn't asked someone prior to this. Before she thought about it further, he asked, "Do you want Heather to come over and stay with Kristy? I think I can get a sitter."

"What time do you think we'll be home?"

Alex shrugged. "Probably around midnight."

"There's a teenager next door who babysits for me. I think it'll be better if Heather just stays here."

Tilting his head, Alex studied her for a few moments. Then he asked, "How long have you been divorced?"

"Three years." She didn't like to talk about her marriage, how she'd felt while she was married, how foolish that she hadn't read Jeff better from the beginning. So she turned the tables. "How about you?" she asked.

Alex straightened. "I've never been married." Standing, he closed the subject. "I'd better get Kristy home."

He'd never been married?

She wondered if he had wanted to marry Kristy's mother, or if marriage was a foreign word to him as it was to a lot of men. Suddenly her decision to go out with him on Saturday night didn't seem to be such a good one. But she had second-guessed herself too much in the past. She wasn't going to start doing it now. One night, one date, wouldn't ruin her life. It didn't even have to complicate her life.

But as Alex called his daughter and Kristy came running to him, Amanda knew he was already complicating her life.

She'd just have to be careful and not do anything impulsive.

When Alex pulled up in front of Amanda's house and braked, he drew a deep breath. He felt like a teenager on his first date. Obviously, Amanda was used to dating. She even had a babysitter on call. He just wished this was as easy for him. His secretary's daughter was staying with Kristy tonight. Georgia had assured him her seventeen-year-old was reliable and dependable, but he'd made sure she had all the emergency numbers as well as his pager number, just in case. He was so used to having his parents as a backup where Kristy was concerned.

Opening his car door, he told himself he shouldn't expect too much from this evening. After all, he and Amanda hardly knew each other. Yet, on the other hand, he felt as if he'd known her a long time. She apparently didn't want to talk about her divorce anymore than he wanted to talk about his relationship with Rhonda. It had been such a mistake, except for Kristy. He'd never considered his daughter a mistake.

Amanda's front door was open, but peering through the screen, he didn't see any sign of movement. So he rang the bell. Heather came running and opened the door. "Mom's almost ready. She's foolin' with her hair. Come on in and wait. I'm going out back. Debbie's gonna paint my nails for me."

He supposed Debbie was the teenager who babysat. Feeling a bit uncomfortable being alone in Amanda's house, he chose a Boston rocker, but immediately stopped rocking when Amanda came down the hall.

She was an absolute knockout. She'd swept her blond hair to the top of her head where it lay in soft curls. A few escaped strands wisped along her cheeks. Around her neck, she wore a simple gold chain that sparkled when she moved and emphasized the creaminess of her skin and the elegance of her profile. And the dress . . . it was black with no sleeves or straps and he wondered what the hell was holding it up. It was covered in tiny beads and molded to her curves perfectly. The side slit showed enough of her leg to make him sweat, and as she walked toward him, he wanted her in a way he hadn't wanted a woman in years.

Coming to his feet, he said, "You look fantastic."

"Thank you. You look pretty sharp yourself."

He'd dressed as he always did for this type of function—charcoal suit, white dress shirt, geometrically designed black and gray tie. But he liked her gaze on him, and he couldn't wait for the first dance when he could hold her in his arms. He had the feeling that dancing with Amanda was going to be an arousing experience. With a smile of thanks for the compliment, he asked, "Are we ready?"

"I'll just say goodnight to Heather and Debbie, then we can go."

The drive to the Bridgeton Center was short, and they hardly had time to get into conversation. Alex asked Amanda if she liked living in Cedar Grove. And she answered that she'd found it a friendly community, for the most part, and a good place to raise Heather. He discovered that she'd moved here from the outskirts of Philadelphia, and that she enjoyed the close-knit community more than the big city.

The parking lot was almost full when they arrived at the Center. "I guess everyone else came for the cocktail hour," he commented.

"Are you looking forward to seeing old friends?" she asked.

He wanted to say he was looking forward to spending the evening with her. Instead he answered, "I keep in touch with friends from school who are still living in Cedar Grove. And the others . . ." He shook his head. "When memories of high school are all you have in common, the conversation ends pretty quickly." With that he climbed out and went around to her side to open her door.

When they went inside, Alex found his name tag on a long table, but he pocketed it instead of pinning it on his jacket.

"Don't want anyone to know who you are?" she teased.

"I'd rather someone looks at my face rather than my lapel," he responded with a smile.

Inside the immense room, crystal and china glimmered on white tablecloths. Many tables were already filled, but as Alex glanced over the area, he saw someone waving to him. "This way," he said to Amanda, guiding her with his hand in the small of her back.

Although Amanda was wearing high heels, she felt small beside Alex as he guided her toward a table. The pressure of his hand on her back was gentle, but it was almost as if she could feel the heat of his hand through her dress. The way he'd looked at her when he first saw her . . . she'd felt beautiful and desirable, in a way she hadn't in a long time. But she kept telling herself she knew very little about this man, even though her heart raced and her skin tingled every time she was near him.

At the table, Alex introduced her to Ted Livingston. "Ted's the loan officer over at Cedar Grove Trust," Alex explained.

Ted shook Amanda's hand. "Alex told me he was coming alone. I guess he wanted you to be a surprise."

Alex looked chagrined for a moment, but then said glibly, "I decided it would be a lot more fun dancing with Amanda than talking to you about old football plays all night."

His friend laughed. "I can see your point." His gaze on Amanda was appreciatively appraising. Ted's sun-bleached blond hair and snapping brown eyes, along with his roguish grin, reminded her more of a truant schoolboy than a loan officer, but neither his smile nor his gaze made her heart flip-flop the way Alex's did.

Two other couples joined them at the table as waitresses set salads at each place. Alex pulled out Amanda's chair for her, and she sat, looking forward to the evening. Conversation around the table became lively, including both anecdotes about school days and updates on children and careers. Amanda listened more than she talked, but she wasn't bored. Every once in a while Alex would explain a comment and draw her into the conversation. The others at the table soon learned she was a teacher with a daughter the same age as Kristy.

They were sipping coffee and eating cheesecake when music began playing. To her surprise, Ted pushed his chair back and came over to stand beside her. "Before Alex monopolizes you for the evening, how about a dance?" She glanced at Alex, but his expression was neutral. Not wanting to insult his friend, she said, "Sure," and accompanied Ted to the dance floor.

Ted was a good dancer, and she had no problems following him. They talked as they danced and she learned that he had never been married. He'd decided building a career was more important than a family, but now he was ready to settle down. He remarked, "It's too bad Alex found you first."

Not wanting to give him the wrong impression, she started, "Oh, but Alex and I aren't—"

"You aren't what?" he asked when she stopped.

"We're not . . . dating."

"Then what's tonight?" Ted asked with a skeptical look.

"Our daughters are friends, and I don't think he wanted to come alone."

Ted leaned back and cocked his head. "Alex isn't afraid of doing anything alone. If he brought you, there's a reason. And I doubt it has anything to do with your daughters being friends."

She really didn't know what to say to that.

"Are you telling me that you're available if I want to ask you out?" he persisted.

Not knowing how she'd gotten into this fix, she also didn't know how to bow out of it gracefully. "I'm not committed to anyone."

He arched a brow. "Well, good. Then maybe I'll give you a call sometime." With that he held her a little closer.

Despite what she'd said to Ted, she was relieved when the dance ended.

When they returned to the table, Alex wasn't there and she supposed he had decided to mingle. Excusing herself, she went to the ladies' room to freshen up. After she returned, Alex was sitting by himself.

As she took her seat beside him, he said, "Ted tells me the two of you might go out sometime." His voice was a little too clipped, a little too even.

"That's not true."

"He didn't ask you out?"

She blushed. "He said he might call."

"And you said?"

"I didn't say anything. What was I supposed to say? Besides, what business is it of yours?"

He gave her a dark look. "Right. What business is it of mine?" They sat there for a few minutes in silence until Alex asked, "Would you like to dance . . . with me?"

She wasn't sure she wanted to dance with anybody ever again, but the thought of being held in Alex's arms was too thrilling to resist in a moment of pique. "Yes, I'd like to dance with you," she said simply.

A few moments later, they stood on the dance floor.

Alex took her hand and wrapped his arm around her. She stiffened, but only until they started moving, only until the slow rhythm of the music became a beat as sure as her heart's. Alex guided her expertly—a firm hold, slight pressure, and a familiarity that felt much too natural. It was as if they had danced together for a lifetime.

When the lights dimmed, Alex seemed to tighten his hold and she settled a little closer. He didn't say a word, and after that song ended and another began, they didn't move apart but continued dancing. As he brought their hands into his chest, his cheek almost touched hers. He wore the same spicy cologne she'd smelled the other day, and she remembered the feel of his hair under her fingertips. She remembered altogether too much. But nothing could keep her from enjoying the moment, from nestling against him, from letting his thighs guide her legs. He was a powerful man, and she felt protected in his embrace. Jeff had made her feel smothered, less than him. She'd vowed she'd never let a man make feel that way again.

But with Alex's heat surrounding her, the brush of his skin a movement away, she forgot about her marriage . . . and Jeff . . . and a vow that didn't seem important right now.

This time when the song ended, faster music took its place. Alex leaned back. "Would you like to go out onto the terrace for a while?"

She wondered if he'd remembered what she'd said about not wanting to make a fool of herself anywhere. "I'd like that."

Alex kept his arm around her as they crossed the dance floor, heading toward a row of French doors. When he opened one, she preceded him outside. The flagstone terrace was empty, dimly lit by torch lights around its perimeter. Suddenly she felt self-conscious—alone out here with him. "I guess most people prefer air conditioning to warm night air."

"And what do you prefer?" he asked seriously. "The stale air in there or the scent of honeysuckle and the glow of moonlight?"

She looked up at the sky, a velvet canvas with a hundred twinkling designs that made the night almost magical. "The moonlight," she said a bit breathlessly as she looked up at him.

As he looked down at her and searched her face, she knew her words were an invitation for him to kiss her. Touching her cheek with his palm, he gently turned her face up to his. His lips weren't gentle; they were possessive. But it was a sweet possession that she gladly surrendered to. When his tongue seductively slid along her lower lip, she couldn't help but want more. Alex's hands caressed her bare shoulders, his thumbs stroking her neck. Her arms went around him, but his suitcoat kept her from feeling any more than his taut muscles. The kiss flared into something as hot and brilliant as one of the stars above them. She was caught up in it . . . caught up in *him* until a sharp beeping brought her speeding back to earth.

Beeping. She couldn't quite figure out—

Breaking the kiss, Alex swore under his breath. "It's my pager."

She stepped back, wrapping her arms around herself, suddenly cold now that he wasn't holding her. Stepping over to one of the dim lights, he checked his pager. "It's my home number. Either Kristy or my babysitter. I've got to get this. Do you want to come with me?"

Still dazed by the kiss, she needed a few moments to herself. "I'll wait here."

Alex hesitated a moment, looked as if he wanted to say something, but then instead opened one of the French doors and went inside.

A light breeze brushed Amanda as she gazed up at the sky, wondering what was happening to her, why her good sense hadn't kept her inside. Making a fool of herself on the dance floor was preferable to making a fool of herself out here. Why had she kissed him again like that, as if nothing else mattered? Alex might be handsome and sexy, but she wasn't interested in an affair, and more than that would be such a risk . . .

The door suddenly opened, and Alex was standing before her again, his expression grim. "It's Kristy. She has a temperature of 102. I've got to get home. I can drop you off first—"

She didn't even have to think about her answer. "I'll come with you, Alex. Maybe I can help."

He looked surprised for a moment, then relieved. "Amanda, she's everything to me. If anything ever happened to her . . ."

Whether Alex Woodsides believed in marriage or not, he obviously loved his daughter very much. She touched his arm in a comforting gesture. "I understand."

"I know you do," he said, his voice husky.

Then he led her through the crowd of people inside as they both worried about Kristy, as they both realized how different their lives would be without their children.

Four

Alex hadn't had much experience with an unselfish woman. Kristy's mother had thought of no one but herself, and that's why she'd given Kristy to him in exchange for a handsome settlement which had included her medical expenses. Since he'd just opened his new law practice, he'd had to take out a loan to pay her. But his child had been worth any sacrifice and still was. Rhonda had given up all rights to a daughter she'd never know so she could pursue her own law career. It was the epitome of selfishness, though he had to be grateful she had gone through with the pregnancy after much convincing on his part.

Amanda, on the other hand, was a caring mother. And the exceptional aspect about her was that she didn't mind extending that caring to *his* daughter.

As he drove past Amanda's house, up the incline to the end of the block and turned into his driveway, a thousand and one reasons for Kristy's fever clicked through his mind. Pressing the garage-door opener, he sped straight into the garage and braked. Amanda didn't wait for him to come around to her side, but got out and met him at the doorway to the house. He unlocked the deadbolt and they went inside.

"We're in here," the babysitter called from the living room.

Alex hurried through the kitchen, Amanda close behind him. When he saw his daughter huddled on the sofa under an afghan on such a warm night, his fears intensified.

"I didn't want Terry to call you," Kristy said morosely. "My stomach's just a little upset."

Fondly, Terry looked down at her charge. "She was dizzy, too."

After picking up the thermometer from the end table, he scooped Kristy up into his arms, afghan and all, and started toward the stairs. "I'm putting you to bed. We'll take your temperature again, and then decide what we're going to do. Terry did the right thing by calling me."

Kristy's eyes glistened. "But I didn't want you to leave early. I wanted you to have fun, and—"

Alex glanced at Amanda. "We did have some fun, and now I'm going to take care of you."

Mounting the stairs, he didn't stop until he reached Kristy's room and settled her in her bed. A few minutes later, he saw her temperature was still 102. Her eyes were glassy. He was considering taking her to the emergency room when Amanda appeared in the doorway.

Coming over to Kristy, she sat on the bed beside her. "Honey, does your stomach hurt at all?"

Kristy shook her head.

"Are you sure?" Amanda asked.

"I'm sure. It just feels icky."

After Amanda took the thermometer from Alex's hand, she saw the reading. When she looked up at him, she said, "It's probably just a twenty-four hour bug."

"That's what my common sense is telling me, but

the other part of me wants to take her to the emergency room."

"Aw, Daddy, not the hospital. Please."

Amanda patted Kristy's leg. "Why don't we get you some soda to sip on?" Her gaze met Alex's. "If she doesn't feel better in a couple of hours, you can always take her to the emergency room then."

From the doorway Terry said, "Mr. Woodsides, if you don't need me anymore, I'm going to drive home."

Alex took out his wallet and went into the hall. He paid and thanked Terry for coming to watch Kristy, then said to Amanda, "If you don't mind staying with her for a few minutes, I'll go get some soda and ice."

Amanda smiled at him. "I don't mind."

After seeing Terry out and making sure she was safely on her way, Alex found decaffeinated soda, poured it over ice and took it upstairs to his daughter. But in the hallway, he stopped. Amanda had moved and was sitting beside Kristy. They were both propped against the pillows. She'd opened a book and was reading in a low voice. Kristy looked so content cuddled up beside her that Alex's heart ached. Did she need a woman's touch more than he thought? *Did* she need a mother? He knew he was a good parent, but was he enough? Especially when it would come to seeing her through her turbulent teen years. With his mother's help, they'd always managed, but maybe managing wouldn't be enough in the future.

When he handed Kristy the soda, she took a tentative sip. "Think you can keep down some acetaminophen?" He wanted to lower that fever.

"Maybe with a cracker?" Amanda suggested.

He should have thought of that.

"I can try," Kristy answered. "I didn't throw up or anything. I just felt like I had to."

Amanda's gentle smile comforted Alex. "If you can't keep them down, we can try a lukewarm bath. That can get your fever down, too."

"Does that really work?" He'd never tried it.

"When all else fails," she answered.

He was glad Amanda was here, and yet felt uncomfortable about being comfortable with it. It didn't make much sense. He supposed it had to do with not easily depending on anyone . . . or trusting anyone, especially with Kristy. His mother was the exception, though when he had made the decision to keep Kristy, even she had thought he was crazy. But he'd known he could never give up his child.

After managing to take a pill and eat a cracker without incident, Kristy's eyes grew heavy-lidded, and she leaned against Amanda's shoulder. "Can you stay for a little bit?" she asked sleepily.

"Amanda has to get home to Heather," Alex told his daughter gently.

"I'm sure Heather wouldn't mind," Kristy argued. "Please. Just a little while?"

Bringing her gaze to Alex's, searching for his reaction, Amanda waited a few moments. But he couldn't tell her he wanted her to stay as much as he wanted her to go. The situation was confusing as all hell!

Apparently deciding on her own, she turned back to his daughter and said, "I'm sure Heather wouldn't mind. Why don't we finish this story, and then I'll tuck you in. Your dad can take over from there. Okay?"

Kristy nodded.

Alex tugged off his tie and shrugged out of his suit coat, laying both across the corner of Kristy's bed.

Then he sat on her bedroom chair, propped his legs up on the bed, and listened to Amanda's soothing voice as she read Kristy one of her favorite stories. He didn't read to his daughter aloud much anymore. He wasn't sure exactly when he'd stopped. But apparently Kristy wasn't growing up as quickly as he thought. Sometimes she acted older than her years, and other times she seemed like a four-year-old again, needing his hugs. He hoped she would always need hugs.

As Amanda had suggested, she finished the story, then tucked his daughter in, pulling the sheet up to Kristy's chin. Alex took his daughter's temperature again and noticed that it had dropped to 101. Maybe this *was* just a bug that would be gone by morning. As he stood by the bed, Amanda leaned down and kissed Kristy on the forehead. The tender gesture touched him deeply.

"I'll see you soon," she told Kristy, then left him with his daughter.

After he hugged and kissed Kristy good night, he joined Amanda in the hall.

"You don't have to come downstairs with me. I can let myself out," Amanda said, looking as beautiful as she had all evening.

"I should have sent you home with Terry." He dug in his pocket for his keys. "Why don't you take my car—"

"Oh, Alex, don't be silly. I have less than a block to walk. I'll be fine."

"I don't like the idea of you walking home alone in the dark.

"I'm a big girl, Alex. And I've even taken a self-defense class."

"Self-defense?" he asked, surprised.

She smiled. "It was my first bid for independence after I got my divorce. Seemed like a good idea, especially living in Philadelphia."

"Have you ever had to use it?"

"No. But that doesn't mean I don't remember how," she said with an amused warning look.

Laughing, he suddenly felt better about Kristy and the evening. "I wish tonight had turned out differently."

"I had a good time while we were there."

"Dancing with Ted Livingston?" he wanted to know.

"No. Having dinner with your friends and dancing with you."

Neither of them mentioned the kiss.

Alex suddenly wanted to make Amanda swear she wouldn't date Ted or anyone else. But he knew he was being irrational. Still, he did want to see her again. "Call me as soon as you get home," he demanded.

Her brows arched. "I'm used to taking care of myself, Alex."

It was a subtle reminder that he had no right to give her any orders. Maybe he had no right, but he wanted the right. And maybe he wanted more. He knew he wanted her in his bed, but Amanda wouldn't be a one-night stand. And he wasn't sure he was ready for anything else.

Rationalizing, he said, "You were my date tonight, and you're my responsibility until you're home safely. Call me, okay?"

When she finally nodded, he wanted to give her a good night kiss that they'd both remember for a long time. But if he kissed her, he'd want more than a kiss and he might forget what was most important in his life—his daughter sleeping in the room next to his.

As Amanda turned to walk down the hall, he wanted to call her back. He wanted to keep her in his house. He wanted to lock her in his room and not come out until the physical need that had been building for years had been satisfied. Instead, he listened to her heels on the treads of the steps. He heard his front door open and close.

Then he went to his room to get ready for bed and to wait for her call.

On Monday afternoon Amanda was cleaning her living room when the phone rang. Stepping down from the stool, window cleaner and paper towels in hand, she hoped it was Alex. She'd called him after she'd gotten home Saturday night. They'd both said good night, and the huskiness in his voice had made her wish the evening hadn't ended so abruptly, though another one of his kisses could lead her into more trouble than she was ready for.

He'd called her again Sunday to tell her Kristy was feeling better and the fever had broken. But he wasn't sure he should bring Kristy over Monday morning because he didn't want Heather to get sick. Amanda assured him that if Heather was going to catch the germ, it had already happened. Then she'd told Alex that she had called Kristy's teacher, and that the woman explained that Kristy had only started having problems with math during the last quarter of the year. Deciding there was no other apparent reason for Kristy's problems, she agreed with Alex that it must have just been some difficulty with one particular math concept.

When Alex said good-bye, assuring her he'd see her

the following morning, Amanda was disappointed. She'd secretly hoped he'd ask her out again. Then chiding herself for behaving like a teenager, she'd occupied herself with other things. This morning he'd been running late when he'd dropped Kristy off. It was possible he was calling now to ask about how his daughter was feeling. As far as Amanda could see, except for eating a little lighter than usual, Kristy seemed to be her old self.

Hurrying into the kitchen, Amanda eagerly picked up the phone.

"Amanda, it's Clara Webb."

She hadn't talked to Clara since their last Career Day meeting. "Hello, Mrs. Webb. I hope you're enjoying your summer."

"I was enjoying it just fine until the letter came in the mail today."

Amanda's mail didn't arrive until late afternoon. "What letter is that?"

"The one Mr. Woodsides sent out to prospective speakers for Career Day. Do you know anything about it?"

"No. I didn't even know he'd sent one out."

"Yes, well it has that 'cc' down at the bottom, so everybody on the committee is getting one. But it's what's *in* the letter that's the problem."

"Since I didn't receive mine yet, you'll have to tell me about it," Amanda responded patiently, knowing Clara often made a mountain out of a molehill.

"Mr. Woodsides promised them a breakfast—a breakfast, mind you. How are we supposed to afford that?"

"For all the speakers?" If they expected to have thirty speakers . . .

"Yes, for all the speakers. That's definitely not in our budget. Last year they came after lunch, and we gave them punch and cookies later, then sent them on their way. Just what are we going to do about this?" Clara demanded. "He already sent these letters out!"

"I'll be seeing Mr. Woodsides later this afternoon. I'll talk to him about it."

"We may have to have an emergency meeting. He might have a lot of energy, but he cannot unilaterally decide how to run this day. We all have a say in that."

For once Amanda was in complete agreement with the older teacher. She assured Clara that she would keep her informed, then went back to her cleaning, not looking forward to confronting Alex.

Later, when Amanda heard the sound of Alex's car in the driveway, she was surprised. He was early for a change, and she was nervous. She shouldn't be. She hated the feeling. It was the way she used to feel with Jeff—worried about doing or saying something he would disapprove of. She'd thought she'd left all that behind her. She shouldn't care whether or not Alex disapproved of what she had to say.

But she did.

Instead of waiting for him to come around to the back where the girls were playing, she opened the front door and motioned him inside. His smile when he stepped over the threshold made her nerves jitter more than ever. By this time her mail had arrived, and she'd seen the letter that had concerned Clara. Deciding to leave the older teacher out of this, she said, "We have to talk."

His smile slipped away. "Isn't Kristy feeling well again?"

"This isn't about Kristy." She picked up the letter

from her coffee table. "You invited participants in Career Day to breakfast. That's not in the budget."

He slid one hand into his trouser pocket, not looking the least bit disturbed. "I know it's not in the budget, but we have to show these people that we value their time—and their expertise—or they won't want to help again. I'm going to pay for it as a community service. I've made arrangements with the small family restaurant down the street from the school. They assured me that they can provide good service and will stay on schedule."

He'd already set up the breakfast. And he was going to pay for it? He was going to take control of this whole project? Over her dead body. "Alex, you can't just do whatever you please. We formed a committee to run ideas past each other. You can't simply take over."

"Why are you so upset? Plans are proceeding smoothly. Everything's under control. I told you I would absorb the cost." He stopped and gave her a probing look. "Or maybe *you* want to run the show."

Amanda had worked on committees time and time again. She knew about working with people—delegating and sharing responsibility—but apparently Alex didn't. "I asked you to head this committee, but not to steamroll over everyone. We're all equals here. We're all on the same team."

"Then just consider me the quarterback," he said with an amused smile that made her angrier, because now he was being condescending.

Holding on to her temper, she said, "In the future, Alex, you bring an idea to the committee before you act on it."

His shoulders suddenly seemed to become broader as his stance became defensive. "And what if I don't?

Volunteers for this job are so easy to come by, aren't they, Amanda?"

"Are you threatening me?"

"With what? Quitting? I don't quit, Amanda. And I don't change the way I'm doing things just because some female can't take a little direction."

So now she was "some female." And if this was giving direction, she hated to see what he would be like if he was really in charge. He had taken over, and that's what irritated her the most.

"This 'female' prefers partnership to dictatorship. Just realize that if you *are* going to take control, everybody else just might let you do it all. Are you ready for that?"

"Are you threatening me?" he asked, eyes narrowed.

"With what? Abdication? Is that what you want? Well, I don't abdicate. I'll be looking over your shoulder, Alex, because I want this day to be a success as much as you do."

"Fine," he said, his jaw set. "Now I'm going to get Kristy and take her home."

Amanda didn't like the way they were leaving this, but he had implied she was an irrational female. And she wasn't about to forget that anytime soon. She didn't follow him as he crossed to the kitchen and went out the back door. And when she heard his car start a few moments later, she couldn't believe tears pricked in her eyes.

She only had one consolation—she'd stood her ground with him.

But that ground didn't feel too steady.

As Amanda made supper for herself and Heather, her argument with Alex weighed more heavily on her mind. She thought about her conversation with Clara Webb; she thought about what she'd said to Alex. Maybe he'd had no right to act without consulting the committee, but she should have handled the situation differently. The more she thought about it, the more uncomfortable she became.

It was almost Heather's bedtime when Amanda called Debbie next door and asked her if she could come over for a while. She told the teenager and Heather that she had to run an errand and would be back in no more than an hour. After Heather promised that she would get ready for bed without stalling, Amanda decided to drive to Alex's house. If he wasn't interested in being amiable again, she could at least drive around for a while and think.

As she alighted from her car and approached Alex's front door, darkness was falling, and the sound of her own heartbeat was entirely too loud. She rang the bell, and a few moments later he opened the door, looking very surprised to see her. His brows arched, and he asked, "Are you still loaded for bear?"

His T-shirt was worn and soft-looking, hugging the muscles of his upper arms. His jeans looked as if they'd seen a hundred washings and fit him so well that . . . She quickly lifted her gaze to his face again. "I'm sorry if I overreacted."

"If?" he asked.

She'd take part of the blame, but not all of it. "I'm not the only one at fault."

After studying her for a long silent moment, he said, "No, you're not. Come on in." Rather than showing her to the living room, he led her into the kitchen and out on to the screened-in back porch where he motioned to a comfortable cushioned glider. After she sat, he sat beside her.

The intimacy of nightfall enfolded them as she settled next to Alex, his knee almost brushing hers. "Where's Kristy?"

"I just tucked her in. She informed me I was a grouch tonight."

Amanda almost smiled. "Were you?"

"Could be," he said with a shrug. "I was trying to figure out the best way to approach you and to—"

"Apologize for your high-handedness?" she supplied.

He grimaced and gave her a wry grin. "Possibly. I had a call from Clara Webb."

"I see," she said softly.

"Amanda, I know how important team work is, but I thought you wanted me to head the committee so I would get things done. That's what I was trying to do."

And maybe she *had* asked him for that reason. She'd known his professional reputation. "I knew you would get things done. But when you took over—"

"I overstepped a boundary you'd set."

"Something like that."

His gaze was probing, but she didn't really want to get into the subject of her marriage.

Apparently Alex had other ideas because he asked, "Did your first marriage end badly?"

Trying to keep the atmosphere light, she quipped, "I don't hate men or anything like that."

"Amanda."

Her name was said with such gentleness that she knew he wanted the truth, that he cared if she'd been hurt. "It ended, Alex. I don't know if marriage can ever end well."

"Why don't you want to talk about it?"

"Because there isn't any point."

"Do you still have contact with your ex-husband because of Heather?"

If anything about her marriage still stabbed her deeply, it was Jeff's attitude toward Heather.

Alex was watching her so carefully that he could apparently see the emotion rising up inside her. "Tell me," he prodded.

"You asked if it ended badly. I filed for divorce. Jeff didn't want it. But I had to get out for my emotional well-being and for Heather's. He became very angry and bitter, and essentially told his lawyer he wanted to cut us out of his life. I agreed not to take child support or alimony—not that I would have gotten alimony because I'm working."

"You deserve child support."

"We don't need it, Alex. We've managed just fine. I wasn't going to force Jeff to do something he didn't want to do. And in a way, I was glad he didn't want to give it. If he had, he would still have expected some kind of control over Heather, maybe even still over me."

"So he turned his back?" Alex asked.

"Yes. And not three months after our divorce, I heard he was engaged and then married. He started a new life very easily, and that makes me wonder how much we meant to him to begin with. When my position in the school district where I was teaching was terminated because of budget cuts, I thought it was the worst possible thing that could happen. Yet deep inside I knew Heather and I would be all right. I got a job as a secretary in an insurance company, and then heard about this teaching position in Cedar Grove.

Moving here was really the best thing for us. It gave us a chance to start fresh."

Alex turned toward her. "I'm glad you moved here."

Soft light spilled from the kitchen onto the darkened porch. Not a leaf stirred and Amanda felt as if she were on the threshold of something terrifically important—something that might change her life again.

Alex slid his hand under her hair, moved his fingers seductively in the silky strands as if he relished the feel. Then he nudged her closer to him. When he touched his lips to hers, her breath caught and her heart raced. She was scared as well as excited. But excitement won over fear, and she opened her mouth to Alex. She could feel Alex's desire surge through her, heightening all her senses, fueling her need as well as his. She hadn't let herself need, not sex . . . and certainly not a man. But somehow Alex had demolished a few of the walls she'd built to fortify herself, to protect herself. As his hands ran through her hair and then cupped her head, she shivered. Just the intense anticipation was enough to make her body quiver. His tongue was hot, first coaxing and then commanding.

Her hands went to his shoulders. His T-shirt was so worn it was almost as if she were touching his warm flesh. But not quite. Her fingertips slid to his neck. She could feel the beat of his pulse, the tension coursing through his body, the arousal that she could sense. She'd dreamt of another kiss, even if she hadn't admitted it during her waking hours. She'd dreamt of more. So in control since her divorce, she now felt totally out of control—wanting Alex, responding to him, giving more than she'd given in a very long time. The desire between them became a craving she had to satisfy. She couldn't seem to get close enough and neither could he. They were both straining against boundaries and inhibitions and against the desire to stay uninvolved.

What would it mean to be involved with Alex? She had Heather to think about, and he had Kristy. They weren't just tampering with their own lives, but their daughters'.

The thought of Heather probably waiting up for her made Amanda slide her hands away from Alex and pull away.

When he looked down at her, she was glad they were sitting in shadows. "I've got to get home. I told the babysitter I'd only be gone a hour."

Alex checked his watch. "You've got at least another fifteen minutes."

The smile playing around his mouth told her he knew exactly what they could do with those minutes, too. But she knew that wouldn't be wise, certainly not any wiser than falling more deeply under his spell.

"What's the matter, Amanda?" he asked. "I want you, and from your reaction, I think you want me. Can't we just be honest enough to say it?"

"I've wanted a lot of things in my life, Alex, but that doesn't mean that they're good for me—or that they're good for Heather."

"We could spend some time alone together without the girls."

"And exactly what do you mean by alone? At a motel? Is that what you want, Alex?"

"It might be a good start," he said, his frustration obvious.

But she shook her head. "We both have to think about this very carefully. I'm not about to mess up my life again, or Heather's." Shifting to the edge of the glider, she stood, and he did, too.

Alex didn't look pleased with her or with what she'd said, but she couldn't help that. As he walked her to the door, she searched for something else to say to him, something that would put them back on a casual footing. But there wasn't anything. When he opened the door for her, she left.

Neither of them said good night.

Five

"Did you and Mrs. Carson have a fight?" Kristy asked as Alex set bags of hamburgers and fries on the kitchen table Wednesday evening.

Alex wished the answer were as simple as yes or no. The last time he'd kissed Amanda, everything had gone a little crazy. He'd always thought he could control his physical desires as easily as he controlled the rest of his life. Goal oriented, he saw what he wanted and went after it. Concentrating on his work and Kristy, he'd always been able to shut out other distractions, including needs that got just too complicated to fulfill.

But since Amanda, his control had slipped away. She made him lose perspective. She made him question things he hadn't questioned before. And when she'd left Monday evening, he realized he *had* decided a motel room would be the answer—a very nice motel room, but a motel room, nonetheless. Only that wasn't what she wanted. Apparently pleasure was low on her list of priorities.

"No, we didn't have a fight," he answered his daughter as he opened the bags.

"But you didn't talk to her—yesterday morning, or last night, or this morning, or tonight. You just dropped me off and picked me up. You didn't even come inside."

Surprised that Kristy had even noticed or cared, he glanced at her, wondering if something else was on her mind, something that she'd wanted him to talk over with Amanda.

Kristy took French fries from a bag and nibbled on one, looking pensive. "Heather's going to a different camp than I am."

So that was it. Last year Kristy had spent a week at an exclusive summer camp in upstate Pennsylvania. Reservations had to be made almost a year ahead. But he knew if he pulled some strings, he might be able to get Heather in the same week as Kristy, even at this late date. He'd do anything to make his daughter happy.

"Do you think Heather would like to go with you?" he asked, already knowing the answer.

"I told Mrs. Carson all about the camp where I went, but Heather told me her mom said it's too expensive. Is it expensive, Dad?"

It was definitely upscale, and he should have thought of that before he said anything. "It is expensive, but . . . let me talk to Mrs. Carson. She's not charging me anything to tutor you or to take care of you while Grandma is gone. Maybe we could make a trade."

After Kristy slid off her chair, she came around and hugged Alex hard. "Oh, Dad, thank you. You're the best."

He was glad his daughter thought so. Now all he had to do was convince Amanda that his latest idea was a good one.

* * *

On Thursday morning Alex arrived at Amanda's house a few minutes early, parked in the drive, and went to the door with his daughter. When Amanda opened it, she looked a little disconcerted. "Oh, hello, Alex."

With awkward tension vibrating between them, Alex asked, "Can I come in for a few minutes?"

Amanda hesitated briefly. "Sure. Is it about the Career Day meeting on Sunday?"

"No. It's about summer camp."

Amanda gave a welcoming smile to Kristy and said, "Go on back to Heather's room. She's cleaning out her closet."

After Kristy had gone down the hall, Alex figured the best thing to do was to get to the point. "Kristy mentioned to me that she and Heather would be going to different summer camps. It would make them happy if they could go together. Since you're not charging me to watch Kristy, I'd be glad to pay for Heather to go to Mountain View with Kristy. I made a call last night, and there have been cancellations, so I can get Heather in. What do you say?"

Amanda had tied her hair back in a ponytail. She was wearing cut-off denim shorts that had fringed and a knit top through which he could see the outline of her bra. She looked totally delectable. But as soon as he made his offer, her blue eyes flashed with silver, and he knew she wasn't going to agree.

"No one pays my bills, Alex. Or Heather's. And that camp is just too expensive for me to afford."

"Look, Amanda, if I had to pay a babysitter for Kristy as well as a tutor—"

"I'm not watching Kristy or tutoring her because I want to get paid for it."

He let out an exasperated sigh. "I know that. But the girls want to be together. And the truth is, last year when Kristy went to camp, I'm not sure she really enjoyed it. She didn't know any of the girls there, and they already had their friends from the year before. I just want her to have a good time."

Amanda's silence lasted more than a few seconds as she assessed him and his motives. Finally she made a suggestion of her own. "Maybe you should tour the camp that I've chosen for Heather. Kristy told me what her camp was like, and Rocky Top doesn't have the same kind of luxurious accommodations, but then I don't believe the girls need anything fancy. They need good supervision, activities they like, and each other's companionship."

For some reason, Alex felt this was some kind of test. Amanda obviously didn't want anyone making decisions for her, and he guessed that was how she saw his offer. He thought about it. Why not check out Rocky Top? After all, he didn't have to send Kristy there. But he could at least make the effort. "All right. We can do that," he agreed. "How long does it take to get to this camp?"

"About an hour."

He did some quick calculating. "What about tomorrow afternoon? I'll have my secretary rearrange my appointments. I can be here by two."

"Maybe we should see if they have room for Kristy before we go visit."

He shook his head. "I want to make sure it's suitable for her first. There's no point in proceeding further if she doesn't like the place." He had his doubts about his daughter's comfort, and a cheaper facility usually meant more rustic accommodations.

"You don't think she's going to like it, do you?"

"I'm withholding judgment until I see the place. She's used to Mountain View and everything it has to offer. It has nice dorms, tile floors and fluffy towels."

Amanda's pretty brows arched. "At Rocky Top, the girls bring their own towels."

He had to smile at her. "And a bedroll?"

"You bet," she answered, challenging him to make something of it.

They practically stood toe-to-toe, defensively, like two wary boxers who'd just entered a ring. Or like two people attracted to each other who didn't want to give into the attraction. With the girls along tomorrow afternoon, they'd have two energetic buffers.

"Can you give me the number for the camp? I'll call and let them know we're coming," he finally said.

"You can if you want, Alex, but they have an open door policy. Anyone can visit anytime."

What she was really saying was that this camp wasn't exclusive. This camp was unpretentious and very different from Mountain View. "I want to call and ask a few preliminary questions. It will give me a feel for the place."

"I'll get you the number." Turning away from him, she headed toward the kitchen. Her ponytail bounced as she walked, and Alex admired her slender figure as well as her spirit. He was already looking forward to tomorrow afternoon.

As Alex drove to Rocky Top the following afternoon, he glanced at Amanda when she spoke to him, when she spoke to the girls, when he stopped for a light, or any other time he thought it was safe. Having her in the car beside him was a distraction, but a distraction that made him feel totally alive and, he had to admit, somewhat aroused even when he wasn't looking at her. When he wasn't looking at her, he could still smell her perfume. He could still remember their kisses. He sensed her beside him, although no part of their bodies were touching. Even as they sang rounds of "Row, Row, Row Your Boat," the sharp awareness of his attraction to Amanda couldn't be denied.

Taking the designated exit from Interstate 81, Alex remembered the directions to the camp printed on the flyer describing the facility. Amanda had given it to him with the phone number. The camp was nestled in the hills, and as Alex turned onto an access road, he realized the scenery here was as picturesque as Mountain View's. But as he caught a glimpse of the camp itself and its buildings, any other resemblance to Mountain View didn't equate. Mountain View had dormitories, Olympic-sized pools indoors and outdoors, well-kept stables and riding trails. This camp looked like . . . well, like a throwback to the sixties. There were ten cabins, and he wasn't sure they looked like they could weather a good storm.

As if she read his mind, Amanda said, "You have to see it up close to appreciate it. And wait until you meet the counselors; they're terrific with the kids."

"Boys *and* girls come to this camp?" he asked, realizing it for the first time.

"Yes, it's co-ed."

"Mountain View is just for girls," he murmured.

"Alex, it's important for children to interact—both sexes. That's how they learn about relationships."

He supposed Amanda was right, but he still liked

the idea of a fortified dorm with all the conveniences and all girls inhabiting it much better.

From the back seat, Kristy tapped him on the shoulder. "Hey, Dad, look! There's a lake over there—and canoes. I've never been in a canoe."

Even though he'd started Kristy in private swimming lessons when she was five, and she was a good swimmer, he didn't know if he liked the idea of her out on the water when he wasn't around.

Amanda nudged his elbow and said in a low voice, "They don't go out in the canoes without life jackets."

That bit of information didn't make Alex feel a whole lot better. As he climbed out of the car, he heard a round of cheers and kids yelling and calling to each other from a field behind the cabins.

"There's a softball field," Amanda explained as they headed toward one cabin larger than all the others that was obviously the office.

The staff was friendly and eager to answer any of Alex's questions. The manager of Rocky Top introduced Alex to a counselor who took them on a tour of all the facilities. She and Amanda conversed easily, discussing group dynamics and the sense of family life that each cabin created among the girls who slept there for the week. In spite of himself, Alex was impressed with the objectives of the camp—the sportsmanship, independence and camaraderie that the activities and the schedule tried to foster.

On closer examination, he saw that the cabins were sturdy and well-maintained. The communal building where the children had meals and worked on arts and crafts projects was immaculate and freshly painted. He'd expected to find fault with something, but he couldn't. Rocky Top wasn't Mountain View—there was no denying that. But it offered its own brand of summer fun.

When they finished the tour, the counselor said to Alex, "If you want to sign your daughter up, just come back into the office. We have two vacancies left for the week after next—the week Heather is coming. We were booked solid, but as usually happens, we had two families cancel. Or if you don't want to decide now, you can give us a call." After shaking his hand and Amanda's, she smiled at the girls and then returned to the office.

There were no high-pressure tactics here, and no sales pitch. The camp was what it was, and he could either choose it or not.

Kristy and Heather gazed up at him expectantly. After saying, "Excuse us," to Amanda and Heather, Alex dropped his hand onto his daughter's shoulder and guided her toward the shade of a tall poplar. "This camp is a lot different than Mountain View."

"I know, Dad, but I like it. Really I do. And I wanna be with Heather."

Not sure if nine-year-olds' friendships lasted longer than a minute or until a disagreement sent them in opposite directions, he asked, "Would you want to come here if Heather weren't coming?"

When Kristy didn't answer right away, he knew she was thinking about it carefully.

Looking around at the cabins once more, the outdoor pool that wasn't quite Olympic-size, the cafeteria that didn't serve meals on top of tablecloths, she nodded. "I think I'll like it here, Dad. Honest. And I really like the idea of Parents' Day."

The counselor had told them that on the last day of the week, parents were invited to join in and compete in specified activities, watching a program at the end of the day that the kids put on themselves.

"All right. If this is what you want, then let's go in and sign you up."

When Kristy wrapped her arms around him and hugged him, Alex felt as if he'd made the best decision on earth. Rejoining Heather and Amanda, he grinned. "She convinced me, but you two have to promise to watch out for each other while you're here. Got it?"

Both girls were beaming and said in unison, "Got it!"

As the girls hurried inside, Amanda took a few steps closer to him. "You've made them very happy."

"And saved myself some money," he joked.

Amanda laughed. "They'll get their money's worth here, Alex. I really investigated the camp before I chose it for Heather. I called parents who'd sent their children. I spoke to the sister of one of my students who'd been a counselor here."

"I should have known better than to judge it on price or a first impression. And the truth is, I don't want Kristy growing up to be a snob. It's just that I felt safe with her at Mountain View, whether it was the best thing for her or not."

"She can be safe here, too," Amanda assured him.

"If it were up to me, I would keep her in a gilded cage all her life. But I know that's irrational. And I know she'll never learn to fly if I do. It's just hard to keep perspective sometimes."

"More than sometimes," Amanda agreed.

At that moment, he felt closer to Amanda than when he had kissed her. Well, almost. And before he thought about it very long, he found himself saying,

"I got a call from my parents last night. They'd just gotten home. Mom's having a picnic tomorrow evening. How would you and Heather like to come along?"

Looking uncertain, Amanda asked, "Are you sure your parents won't mind?"

"They'd love it. Mom likes to feed a crowd, and Dad likes to show off as the greatest barbecuer on earth."

"Can I bring anything?"

"Just yourself." Then he added, "And Heather."

The door to the office swung open, and Kristy called to him, "Hey, Dad, are you comin'?"

"Coming," he called back, then mounted the wooden steps with Amanda, much too pleased she had accepted his invitation, hoping his parents wouldn't read too much into it.

After all, it *was* only a picnic.

Alex's parents lived in a beautiful stone home in a pretty section of town. Tall maples and elms lined the streets, and pink and blue hydrangea bloomed in profusion along many of the houses. It was a neighborhood that had been developed in the fifties and had seen renovation as well as change. It gave Amanda a solid feeling. Alex had come from this middle-class background. It was much different from hers.

Growing up, she'd lived in an apartment with her mother in a poor section of town. Her father had left before she was old enough to remember him very well. Like Jeff, he'd never looked back. He hadn't cared that he had a daughter. The school guidance counselor had helped Amanda find every scholarship and grant available for her to attend college. When

Amanda's mother died during her sophomore year, she'd taken an apartment in the small college town and worked two jobs, determined to make a success of her life. And when she'd met Jeff, she'd thought she'd have the family she'd always dreamed of. But Jeff's idea of family and hers had been very different. She'd wanted a husband who made his family a priority, but Jeff had found almost everything else more important. Yet he'd still wanted to dictate her every move—and Heather's.

Amanda was curious about Alex's parents and how he'd been raised. As his parents welcomed her on the covered patio of their home, she knew her curiosity was about to be satisfied.

After Amanda introduced her daughter to Doris and Ed Woodsides, Kristy took Heather into the house to show her the room where she stayed when she slept overnight.

As Amanda gave Doris a box of imported chocolates that she'd brought as a hostess gift, Doris winked at her son. "This young lady has good taste."

"Yes, she does," Alex agreed with a smile at Amanda.

Ed waved in the direction of the grill. "Let's get these hamburgers grilled, boy. Doris, bring out all those condiments you've got in the refrigerator. Give us twenty minutes and we'll be ready."

It seemed Alex had gotten his take-charge attitude from his father. Amanda followed Doris into the kitchen, and they chatted easily. She found Alex's mother very comfortable to talk to. As Amanda helped Doris fix a vegetable plate, the older woman asked, "Are you and Alex just friends?"

Remembering their passionate kisses, the way she

felt when he touched her, their one date that had been cut short, Amanda hedged. "I'm not sure."

Doris shook her head. "If my son isn't careful, he's going to turn into a cranky old bachelor."

Amanda laughed. "I don't know about the bachelor part, but I haven't found him too cranky."

Alex's mother smiled, but the smile slipped away as she said, "Rhonda hurt him deeply. I'm not sure how serious they were, but the idea that she didn't want their baby and could walk away because a child didn't fit in with her plans, killed any feelings he might have had for her."

"He hasn't told me much about it," Amanda said honestly, not wanting Doris to reveal confidences that might make Alex uncomfortable.

"Well, he should. Maybe if he talked about it, he'd get over it. Kristy needs a mother, and he needs . . . well, more than Kristy and his work."

"It's difficult to trust again," Amanda admitted.

"Sometimes you just have to take the leap," Doris said sagely.

Amanda wondered about that leap as they took the food outside. Alex came over to her and stood very close. "Did Mom talk your ear off?"

Wearing a white polo shirt and navy shorts today, he was tall and male, and she liked being near him. "Not quite," she answered with a smile.

His gaze passed over her one-piece coral culotte outfit. As if he couldn't keep from touching her, he fingered the collar near her hair. "You're being diplomatic. Mom can grill better than any member of the Spanish Inquisition, and you don't even know she's doing it."

"I like her, Alex. I didn't mind answering her questions. She just wants to get to know any woman you might be keeping company with."

At that he grinned and draped his arm around her shoulders. "Come on, let's go find the girls. It's time to eat."

Conversations criss-crossed each other throughout the meal. When Amanda complemented Ed Woodsides on his barbecuing ability, Alex acted affronted. And Ed beamed. Alex murmured in her ear, "You know how to score points."

She laughed, but the feel of Alex's breath on her neck, his shoulder pressed against hers, flustered her and she dropped her fork. Alex retrieved it for her, and his eyes glimmered with the knowledge that they wanted more than a few touches or kisses. She sighed. The idea of a motel room was becoming more and more tempting.

After Doris served strawberry shortcake, Ed stood at his place. "This is probably the best time to tell you our news."

Alex looked perplexed. "What news?"

"We're going to put the house up for sale and, come October, we're moving to Florida."

Silence met his announcement as if no one knew quite what to say. Ed's gaze on his wife, he continued, "We can't take the cold winters as well as we used to."

"But, Dad, it's only for a couple of months—" Alex started.

Ed held up his hand. "It's not just the cold, though that's a big part of it. We really like the senior community we visited down there. We're getting older, son, and I don't want to end up in a rocking chair. We can buy a little bungalow and have activities fifty yards away. They have a dance once a week with the kind of music your mother and I like. So we're going to do it. Of course, we'll come up here and visit you and Kristy, and you and Kristy can come visit us."

"But I won't see you all the time," Kristy complained.

Doris patted her granddaughter's hand. "But when you do see us, it will be special. And you can come down and stay without your dad if you want."

"It's a lot to absorb," Alex said, glancing at his daughter.

He had gone very still beside Amanda, and she could tell by the change in his voice that he didn't welcome this news.

When Ed took his seat again and they continued with dessert, he went on to explain all the advantages of living in a warmer climate. But most of all, he and Doris repeated the merits of being near friends their own age and a community that understood older people's needs.

Alex had become quiet and remote, though Kristy asked tons of questions, and Amanda could see that even she was liking the idea of visiting her grandparents in Florida. But as she helped Doris clear the picnic table and load the dishwasher, Amanda could tell that Alex was unsettled. Where before their conversation had been lively, now it drifted into lulls and soon Alex said, "I have some paperwork I have to go over tonight. We'd better go."

After Amanda thanked the Woodsides for their hospitality, Alex drove her home. "Do you want to come in?" she asked Alex, wondering if he needed to talk.

"Can we, Dad? We don't have to stay long," Kristy said.

"Just for a little while."

As the girls ran around to the back yard, he and Amanda followed them more slowly. "You don't like the idea of your parents moving, do you?" Amanda asked.

"It's not a matter of liking," he said. "I just can't imagine them selling the house and leaving behind all the memories that are there."

"They want to try a new life," Amanda responded softly.

"I just hope it's not an impulsive decision they're going to regret. And I've heard horror stories about retirement communities. I'm going to make sure I investigate this one for them. It's too easy to get swindled these days. Besides, Kristy's going to miss them . . ."

"You'll miss having your mother here to watch her."

He frowned. "Do you think that's all I'm worried about—how this is going to inconvenience me?"

Anger was evident in his tone, and Amanda realized he wasn't ready to admit how much he was going to miss his parents. "Alex, no. But their moving does cause some problems."

"I can hire someone to watch her," he grumbled.

"But it has to be someone you can trust."

She'd wanted to ask him more about Kristy's mother, about his relationship with her and exactly what had happened, but she knew now wasn't the time. They paused along the carport in front of a climbing rosebush. The crimson blooms sent a heady fragrance into the evening air.

He dug his hands into his pockets. "I'll find out if Mom wants to spend the summer watching Kristy or if she'll be too busy packing."

"Alex . . ." Amanda said softly, laying a gentle hand on his arm.

"I'm sorry, Amanda. I'm lousy company tonight."

As he gazed down at her, she had no idea what he was thinking—about her, about them. Or even if he was thinking about the two of them at all. And when he spoke, his voice was slightly guarded. "I'll just get Kristy and we'll go. I'll let you know at the meeting tomorrow about keeping her. And about tutoring . . . do you think Kristy needs more sessions?"

Amanda shook her head. "I was going to talk to you about that tonight. Her last few work sheets have all been correct. I don't think she needs any more help."

"I want to thank you for everything you've done for her, Amanda."

"That's not necessary."

He looked at her as if he wanted to say more, but he didn't. He moved away from her and walked toward the back yard.

Amanda felt as if something had changed between them, something that only Alex knew about, and she would have no idea what it was until he told her.

Six

On Wednesday, the fifth of July, Alex drove Kristy to the baseball field at the edge of town. The fireworks display had been postponed because of rain the evening before. After he parked on the grass amid rows of cars, they waved and said hello to the people they knew milling about. Alex bought a soda from a concession stand while Kristy decided on cotton candy. Most of the citizens of Cedar Grove had brought blankets and lawn chairs to enjoy the annual event.

As Alex spread his blanket on the grass, Kristy tugged on his arm. "Dad, there's Heather and her mom. Let's go sit with them."

Alex hadn't had any contact with Amanda since the Career Day meeting on Sunday. Before the meeting he'd told her that his mother wanted to watch Kristy for the rest of the summer, and that conversation had been brief. During the planning session, Amanda's smile had made his pulse race crazily. But ever since his parents had announced their plans to move, he'd decided to cool things off with Amanda and think. Something about his parents leaving had opened old wounds. He didn't know why he was equating his parents' departure for Florida with Rhonda walking out of his life. But he was. Life could change faster than the sun could rise, and he wasn't sure he wanted to get involved more deeply with Amanda. Yet that's where they were headed if they kept seeing each other.

As he raised his gaze to find her in the throng of people, he mentally prepared himself for the sight of her. But he wasn't prepared to see her engaged in a animated conversation with . . . Ted Livingston! His former high school classmate was pointing to something in the distance, and Amanda was smiling and nodding. Heather sat on a blanket beside them, looking none too happy.

So Livingston had made his move! And it looked as if Amanda was glad of it.

Why shouldn't she be? a taunting voice in his head asked. *She tried to be friendly before, during and after the meeting at your house, and you were simply polite.*

So polite, he thought, that she'd looked a little hurt when she'd left. He'd told himself that they'd merely shared a few kisses, and it was his right to call a halt if that was what he wanted. Apparently she'd gotten the message clearly.

Capping his daughter's shoulder, he said, "I think Mrs. Carson's busy this evening. Why don't we just sit here and enjoy the fireworks on our own?"

Kristy looked terribly disappointed, but this time there was nothing he could do about it. As he settled on the blanket and urged his daughter to do the same, he purposefully kept his gaze away from Amanda's direction. He was here to enjoy the fireworks, and that was exactly what he was going to do.

When the phone rang the night after the fireworks, Amanda and Heather were watching a video and dipping into a bowl of freshly made popcorn. Heather stopped the movie as Amanda went to the kitchen to answer the phone. Part of her still hoped it was Alex every time it rang. But when she picked up the receiver and said hello, the masculine voice didn't belong to the man down the street. It belonged to Ted Livingston.

"Hi, Amanda, it's Ted. I just thought I'd call to see if you'd like to go out to a movie this weekend. We could get dinner someplace first—"

She had run into Ted at the fireworks, and he had sat with them to watch the display. During the gorgeous explosions of color and light, she couldn't help but imagine sitting there with Alex rather than Ted. Although Kristy was still in and out of the house in the evenings, Amanda hadn't seen Alex since the Career Day meeting, and then he had acted like a polite neighbor, not like the man who had kissed her senseless. He had been sending her the message that whatever they'd shared hadn't meant anything to him. Maybe he'd been friendly to her, more than friendly, to make sure she kept taking care of Kristy while his parents were gone.

She didn't know what to think any more. She felt confused by his attitude, and more than a little hurt. But she'd get over it. Ted Livingstone didn't make Amanda's heart beat any faster, but he was a nice man. Still, she didn't want to lead him on. "This is a bad week, Ted. I'm taking Heather to summer camp on Sunday, and we're busy getting things organized and just spending time together."

"How long will she be gone?"

"A week."

"Then why don't we do something while she's

gone? How about next Friday night? We can go to dinner, catch a movie. What do you think?"

Since her divorce, Amanda hadn't dated at all, and with Alex, they'd hardly even had a real date . . . alone, just the two of them. She could sit around, moping over Alex's change in attitude, hoping he'd call, but that would be futile. And she would miss Heather next week. Terribly. A date with Ted would give her something to look forward to and help her pass a lonely evening. "All right, Ted. Next Friday night sounds good."

"I'll pick you up around seven. Take care, Amanda. I'll see you then."

When Amanda hung up the phone, she decided she'd just taken her first step in forgetting about Alex Woodsides.

The temperature had climbed into the 90's, but that didn't squelch Heather's enthusiasm for her week at camp. Amanda climbed the ladder and spread her daughter's bedroll over the top bunk in her assigned cabin. "Are you sure you want the top?" she asked Heather.

There were four girls in each cabin. Two of them had already been in and out with their parents and were now heading over to the communal building for orientation. They seemed like nice girls, but Amanda knew Heather was looking forward to Kristy's arrival.

"Kristy wants the bottom bunk, and I like sleeping on top. It'll be fun climbing up and down the ladder."

"Just be careful."

"Please don't say it again, Mom."

Amanda had been giving her daughter safety tips and mentioning "do's and don'ts" for the past week.

Suddenly the screen door on the cabin swung open, and Kristy came barreling in with her sleeping bag. Alex followed close behind with what looked like a heavy duffel bag.

On the ladder, her arms stretched as she smoothed out Heather's bedroll, Amanda felt self-conscious, and she straightened. She couldn't ignore Alex's gaze passing from her feet, up her legs, over her knit top, to her face. And she felt herself blushing. Damn the man. *You're on your way to forgetting him, remember,* she chided herself.

Kristy tossed her state-of-the-art sleeping bag onto the bottom bunk and sat down beside it. "Isn't this just too cool, Dad?"

He ran his hand across his brow. "Actually, it's pretty hot. Are you sure you're going to be able to sleep at night without air conditioning?"

"I'll be fine, Dad," Kristy told him patiently.

Awkwardness filled the cabin as no one spoke. "Hello, Amanda," Alex said.

Finished with fixing the bedroll, she climbed down the ladder carefully. All she needed was to fall on her face in front of him. "Hello, Alex." She didn't have anything else to say, and it was obvious neither did he.

Heather filled the gap. "We'd better get over to the dining hall, don't you think?"

Crossing to the door, Kristy agreed. "Yeah, we don't want to be late."

Amanda picked up the purse she'd laid on Kristy's bunk and followed the two girls out the door. Although Kristy and Heather chattered happily about all the things they were going to do for the next week,

Amanda and Alex were silent. When they reached the dining hall, she saw that folding chairs had been set up in the empty area in the back of the room. Parents and their children had filled in the rows. Kristy and Heather went ahead and found four chairs. To Amanda's dismay, the girls sat on either end, which left her in the middle with Alex. Both of them made sure no part of their bodies touched.

She had never felt more awkward.

Not a bit of breeze stirred through the long screens, and Amanda's shirt stuck to her back. Feeling perspiration at her temples, she pulled a scrunchie from her purse, and gathered her hair into a ponytail. With it off of her neck, she felt a little cooler. That helped her composure as her arm accidentally brushed Alex's. Her gaze met his, and her throat suddenly got tight. What had she done wrong? Why was he acting so distant? But those were questions her pride kept her from asking. She looked away, trying to concentrate on bits of conversation floating around her or just the chatter of the children. She wished they'd get the orientation under way. She wasn't anxious to leave Heather, but she would be glad to get this over with and escape Alex's presence.

"We saw you at the fireworks," he suddenly said.

She supposed making small talk would be easier than sitting there in the tension. "Did you? The next day, Heather told me that Kristy was there, but I didn't see you."

"You were busy. With Livingston."

The tone of Alex's voice puzzled her. Certainly, he couldn't be jealous. Yet, if there was the slightest possibility . . . "We enjoyed the fireworks together."

"I see."

"With Heather gone this week, he thought I'd enjoy going to a movie on Friday. I'm looking forward to it."

Alex gave her a long look, then crossed his arms over his chest and stared straight ahead.

So much for small talk being better than tension!

Finally the activities coordinator stepped up to the microphone. After explaining the daily schedule, rules and regulations, she talked about Parents' Day next Saturday, encouraging all the parents to join in the activities with their children. After asking the parents to take their children back to their respective cabins where they could say good-bye, she closed the session.

Back at the cabin, Kristy and Heather met their counselor for the week, and Amanda felt tears prick in her eyes. It was so hard to leave Heather here. But she knew it was good for both of them. Finally when it was time to go, she said, "Use the phone card and call me whenever you want."

"Mom, I'm gonna be busy. Is it okay if I don't call?"

Amanda smiled. "Yes, it's fine."

Amanda saw Alex slipping Kristy some money to tuck away safely. She had already done that. After giving their daughters hugs, she and Alex headed for the parking lot.

She wanted to talk to Alex as she had before. She wanted to tell him how much she was going to miss her daughter. But he didn't seem open to conversation. Still, they weren't strangers, either. As she motioned to her car, she said, "I'm over there."

He stopped beside her for a moment. "I'm parked at the other end. I guess I'll see you on Parents' Day."

"I guess so." There was nothing else to say, so she

walked toward her car until she heard his voice over her shoulder. "Good-bye, Amanda."

Facing him, she responded, "Good-bye, Alex."

As she opened her car door, she felt very sad. Something had ended, and she didn't know why.

Parents' Day at Camp Rocky Top looked like chaos. But Alex realized it was organized chaos. When he arrived a little after noon and received his schedule of events, he realized he'd be paired with his daughter most of the day. That was fine with him. He hoped they didn't run into Amanda too often. Thinking about her dating Ted Livingston made his blood boil. Most of the day while he kept busy, he could forget about her. Yet at night when he lay in the dark staring at the ceiling, all he could think about was her smile, the softness of her skin, the silkiness of her hair, and the sensual pleasure of her kisses.

But he just wasn't sure he was ready to open himself and Kristy up to the possibility of getting hurt again. What if it didn't work out with him and Amanda? What if she walked away like Kristy's mother had? The pleasure of having a woman in bed beside him every night wasn't worth the complications it might cause.

Kristy led Alex to the field where the relay races were going to take place, and he realized trying to forget about Amanda would be impossible. Apparently the teams were arranged according to the girls' cabins and he, Kristy, Amanda and Heather were on the same team. He couldn't help glancing at Amanda often. She wore a pink tank top and white shorts that left enough bare to more than whet his appetite. She wore her hair in a ponytail again, and the style made her look younger and very desirable. But she didn't look his way whenever he looked in her direction. She was ignoring him, and it annoyed him. Had Livingston kissed her after the fireworks? What about after their date last night? And had she responded with as much fire as with—

That line of thought would drive him crazy. So as best he could, Alex concentrated on the relay races—first a sprint with a baton, then a three-legged race with a burlap sack. When it came time to toss water balloons, he almost looked forward to getting wet in the afternoon heat. But after a few tosses, the balloon landed at Kristy's feet and neither of them got the benefit of a cooling splash.

The parents and children had a choice on the next activity. They could either join a group for a nature walk or explore caverns on the west boundary of the property. Kristy wanted Alex to see the caves she'd toured earlier in the week. And as they began their trek across the softball field, Amanda and Heather joined their group. Three counselors led them at an easy pace.

As they walked, Kristy gave Alex a play-by-play of everything she had seen and done that week. When he glanced at Heather talking animatedly to Amanda, not far behind them, he guessed that she was doing the same. It was obvious the girls had had a terrific time. This camp had been a good choice, and he owed Kristy's successful week to Amanda's insistence that lots of money didn't always buy the best.

They hiked into a hilly area, and Alex could see mountains rising up ahead of them. Soon he saw the counselors stop at the cave's entrance. Less than half of the campers and their parents had joined this group, most preferring the nature hike. He watched Amanda as she approached the cave, and he saw her hesitate. Some sixth sense that kicked in where she was concerned told him she'd rather not go inside. But then she gazed down at her daughter, and a look of determination came over her pretty face. He guessed she'd do anything in her power for Heather, just as he would do anything for Kristy.

When they stepped inside the cave, the counselors handed each one of them a flashlight from a box on the cave floor. Alex noticed the cooler temperature immediately as one of the counselors who served as a guide explained that the caverns were a constant fifty-two degrees. It felt good to get in out of the hot sun. Their flashlights created both light and shadows as the children played them up and down the walls, and they entered a series of chambers. When he looked back at Amanda, she was standing quite still, and he could swear she closed her eyes. But they soon moved on, and she laid her hand on Heather's shoulder.

In one chamber, damp drops from above deposited calcite, one grain at a time, onto stalagmites on the floor. Flowstone slipped down the walls, creating formations that almost looked like pictures. The children pointed out imagined shapes of birds and animals they'd found earlier in the week. Kristy told him they weren't supposed to touch the formations on the walls because the oil from skin formed a barrier that prevented the flowstone from making further pictures.

When the group moved into a larger chamber that had been dubbed "Community Hall," Amanda and Heather somehow ended up beside him. As he glanced at Amanda, she nervously fiddled with her flashlight. He let her and Heather precede him through a stone hall that led to a smaller space. Before them lay a pool of pure crystal water. Stalactites above reflected in its surface, making it seem deep and mysterious. But Kristy told him there was only about three-inches of water there. He was amazed at the amount of information she'd absorbed about the different types of minerals and rocks that she could now identify. Though he listened, he was all too aware of Amanda in front of him. He saw her rub her arms, and he wondered if she was cold.

Nothing about the caves had seemed dangerous or daunting up to this point, but he sensed a jitteriness about Amanda that was uncharacteristic. The counselor stopped them before they entered another hallway, explaining that the floor was sandy, and there were ropes along the sides. They should be careful and walk single file so they would all stay safe. Alex realized the inside of the cave would be blacker than the deepest night if they didn't have their flashlights. Everyone shone their beams straight ahead so they could see exactly where they were going. Kristy was ahead of him, and Amanda was ahead of her. The group thinned out as the hallway led into four separate chambers.

Heather headed for the left, and said, "Wait until you see this, Mom. It's so cool. But you have to duck your head—"

Suddenly Amanda stopped at the entrance to the small chamber, and as Alex lifted his flashlight to see what had halted her, he saw her face.

"I can't, Heather. I can't go in there."

"But, Mom . . ."

Amanda looked stricken, and Alex immediately knew what was going on. He said to Kristy, "Take

Heather and go over to the counselor. We'll meet you outside."

"But, Dad . . ."

"Do what I said, Kristy. Amanda doesn't feel well. I'm going to take her outside."

Heather looked up at Amanda. "Mom?"

"Go with Kristy over to the counselor, Heather. I'll be fine. Really. I'll be fine." Her words were rushed, and she didn't look fine.

Alex nudged Heather and Kristy to the other chamber and saw Amanda make a mad dash ahead of him back the way they had come, through children and the other parents.

"Amanda," he called, but she kept going.

Determined to keep up with her, he wove in and out of the group until finally she was running a few feet in front of him.

"Amanda, be careful," he warned. But almost as soon as the words came out of his mouth, she tripped and fell hard, her flashlight flying away from her. When she tried to get up she winced, and she would have kept hobbling forward except Alex stopped her.

"Alex, I have to get out of here," she said, real fear in her voice.

"I know," he murmured, sweeping her up into his arms and carrying her swiftly through the caverns, his flashlight guiding his way.

Alex's heart pounded. He couldn't bear the thought of Amanda being afraid or hurt. He could feel the tension and panic in her body and suspected she was holding her breath and trying not to cry. Holding her protectively against him, he could feel the beat of her heart.

Finally he burst through the cave's entrance into

the startlingly bright sunshine. Stopping a few feet away from it, he didn't put Amanda down. He felt her take a few deep breaths. Finally, her blue eyes found his, her face turned red, and she pushed against him so he'd let her down.

But he decided he wasn't about to let her go. Not yet. His head dipped to hers, his lips covered hers, and he kissed her fervently. The kiss was filled with everything he couldn't say, everything he needed to say, everything he didn't want to say.

This time she broke away and pushed at his shoulders again. Instead of looking panicked, she looked very indignant and confused. "You don't call, you don't come around for two weeks and then you kiss me as if—"

"As if that's all I've been thinking about for two weeks?" he finished.

One of the counselors emerged from the cave with Kristy and Heather, all of them looking worried until they saw Amanda in Alex's arms. Then the two girls grinned.

Heather asked, "Are you okay, Mom?"

"I'll be fine if Alex puts me down," she mumbled.

But Heather noticed her mom's leg. "You're all scraped up."

"I tripped as I was hurrying to get out. I'm sorry, Heather. I just got . . . claustrophobic in there. It hit me all of a sudden."

"It's okay, Mom. We saw most of the cave. And besides—" She looked up at Alex. "It's neat that Mr. Woodsides saved you."

Alex chuckled at Amanda's expression of dismay, but then seriously in a low voice he said, "We have to talk, Amanda. But I think it would be better if we did it later, somewhere quiet when everybody isn't watching."

She was stiff in his arms, and her cheeks were still rosy. "I think it's going to have to be a very *long* talk," she concluded.

As he set her on her feet, he couldn't help but smile, and it was the first he'd really felt like smiling since the barbecue at his parents' house. Something had happened in the caverns when he'd seen Amanda panic and then fall, when he'd scooped her up and held her protectively. Holding her so close, he realized how much he'd missed her smiles and her soft voice, her caring attitude, and everything else about her. He had been denying himself the pleasure of her company for reasons that now didn't seem to carry very much weight.

He hoped he could explain it all to her and he also hoped she'd let him.

Walking back to the campground beside her, she avoided his gaze. But he caught her glance at him once when she thought he wasn't looking. She hobbled slightly, and he bet her knee hurt like hell—it had taken the brunt of her fall. Yet she didn't complain.

Heather ran ahead of them, leading them to her cabin. He followed Amanda inside. When she sat on Kristy's bunk, she still avoided direct eye contact, her hands going to her calf and rubbing it.

"Let me look at your knee," he said.

When his hands went to her calf, she practically jumped away from him. "Alex—"

"I want to see how bad it is."

She met his gaze then. "All right," she murmured.

The curve of her calf in his palm tempted him to

do more than examine her knee. But he sucked in a breath and gave her his opinion. "You're going to have to scrub it so it doesn't get infected. You fell on loose gravel."

The screen door opened, and a counselor came in with another woman. "This is our resident nurse. Would you like her to examine you?"

Sliding to the edge of the mattress, Amanda shook her head. "I just need an antiseptic and some good soap. I'll be fine. I'm sorry I panicked like that. It's never happened before."

The counselor looked at Amanda. "Have you ever been inside a cave before?"

When Amanda shook her head that she hadn't, Alex just wanted to pull her into his arms and carry her off somewhere. He wanted to be alone with her, explain to her, kiss her . . . but all of that would have to wait. Parents' Day wasn't over.

With no opportunity to really clear the air, Alex felt a wariness emanating from Amanda the rest of the afternoon and evening. After she took care of her knee, using the antibiotic cream and a bandage that the nurse provided, he stuck close to her throughout the cookout, as did the girls. Since the dining hall had been set up for the program, the campers and their parents sat at weather-worn picnic tables under tall maples. After eating a hamburger, Amanda started to rise from the bench and winced.

"What do you need?" he asked her.

"I was just going to get another glass of punch."

"I'll get it for you. Stay put."

"Alex, I'm not an invalid."

"I didn't say you were. A man can get a woman a glass of punch, can't he?" he teased.

But her answer was guarded. "I suppose so."

After they ate, the girls ran off to get ready for the program. Eventually he and Amanda made their way into the dining hall, and he sat beside her on one of the folding chairs. She didn't try to make conversation and neither did he. Too many people were milling about. But he caught her glancing at him again, and he hoped she wasn't too hurt or angry to listen to what he had to say.

The parents applauded when the children gathered on the makeshift stage. The program began with them all singing a camp song. After that each child had chosen something special to do for the program. Several of them lip-synched to their favorite song. A few of the girls did short dance routines. When Kristy read a poem she'd written about what she'd seen in the woods, describing the lake, explaining how she'd made new friends, Alex's throat tightened. Heather told jokes, while a counselor held up cue cards. The audience laughed at the appropriate places, and Amanda clapped proudly as her daughter took a bow. After the program, Kristy and Heather said good-bye and hugged all the friends they had made. Then Alex and Amanda grabbed duffel bags and walked the girls to the parking lot.

"Will you be okay to drive?" Alex asked Amanda.

"I'll be fine. Fortunately I only need my left leg for walking, not for driving."

At least she was joking with him, at least she wasn't avoiding looking at him. "Can I come in for a few minutes when we get back? Unless you're too tired . . ."

"I'm not too tired," she responded with a slip of a smile.

He breathed a sigh of relief. "Good. I'll see you in a little while then."

Hoping she'd have a few minutes to change her clothes, Amanda saw that she didn't as Alex's car drove up in front of her house. He'd managed to follow her most of the way, even though traffic on the interstate had been heavy. It was as if he didn't want to let her out of his sight. She didn't understand what had happened today, any more than she understood his attitude for the past two weeks. If he thought they could just pick up where they'd left off . . .

Except she wasn't even sure where that was.

Kristy jumped out of Alex's car and ran across the yard as Amanda put her key in the lock and opened her front door. The inside of the house was hot from being closed up all day, even though she'd left the windows open. But Kristy and Heather went back to Heather's room, not seeming to mind.

When Alex stepped inside, Amanda said, "We can sit out on the porch."

He nodded and followed her through the kitchen and out the back door. When she sat on the swing, he sat beside her. The rosebush by the corner of the porch was in bloom, and its fragrance wafted toward the swing. As a hint of night air stirred, a car door slammed a few houses away, and Amanda could count each beat of her heart.

"I'm not sure how to explain," Alex began, sitting close, but not quite touching her.

She stayed completely still because she had no idea where this was going or what he was going to say. She was afraid to let her hopes take off again.

At her silence, he shifted on the swing. "It's complicated, Amanda. Something happened to me when my parents said they were moving to Florida. I'm not sure what. I'm going to miss them. Kristy is, too. I hate the idea of them selling the house where I grew up, but I know that's illogical because they have to do what's right for them. And Kristy and I are getting used to the idea. We've even convinced each other it will be fun to visit them in Florida and have them visit us for a change. The thing is—their announcement acted like some kind of trigger. It reminded me of Kristy's mother, and how easily she walked away and gave up her own child. And suddenly the risk of getting involved with *you* just seemed too great."

He was trying to tell her his turning away from her hadn't been personal, and yet it was . . . very personal. "Caring about anyone is a risk, Alex."

"I know that. And I'm sorry if I hurt you. I never meant to. I thought not seeing you would be the best thing for all of us."

She knew she had to be honest with him. "It did hurt, Alex. One minute you were kissing me as if—" She stopped, embarrassed and amended, "One minute you were asking me to meet your parents and the next you were treating me like a total stranger."

Reaching out, he captured her hand in his. When she didn't pull away, his shoulder brushed hers. "I don't want to treat you like a stranger. I don't want you dating Ted Livingston. I want—"

She waited, holding her breath.

"I want time alone with you. I want to take you to the movies, and to dinner, and to concerts. But most of all—"

She felt him turn toward her, and as his hand caressed her cheek, she leaned toward him.

"I want to kiss you, and hold you, and court you. And, eventually, make love to you. But only when you're ready."

"Oh, Alex." Tears filled her eyes, and she realized how hard it was for him to say all this. "I've missed you," she said softly.

When his mouth covered hers, she realized how much he'd missed her, too. The touch of his lips, the taste of his tongue drove the days of separation out of her mind. How could she not let him back into her life? How could she not understand his fear of giving his heart away? He only needed to know if he could trust her. After all, neither of them wanted to get hurt again.

There was something she had to tell him. When she pulled away from him, he asked, "Am I too late?"

She shook her head vigorously. "No, Alex. And that's what I want you to know. I didn't go to the fireworks with Ted. He was just sort of there. *I* was just sort of there. So we watched them together. When he asked me out for Friday night, I knew I'd be missing Heather, and I was still angry with you. So I said yes. And he's a pleasant man, but he could never be more than a friend."

"Did he kiss you?" The huskiness in Alex's tone said he cared if the other man had.

"No, he didn't. He didn't even try."

"Then he's a fool," Alex murmured as he bent his head to hers again and took her lips with a possessiveness that excited her.

As the kiss became flagrantly sensual, fueling desire and fantasies, and maybe even future dreams, Alex scooped her onto his lap, careful not to hurt her knee. The feel of his arousal under her thigh was enough to send a tremor through her body. He must have felt it because his tongue explored more seductively and his hands became more daring. Lifting her knit top, he reached under it and caressed her midriff. Shivers broke out on her arms as his hand rose higher, closer to her breast. He was right below it, and then circling it in a slow taunting motion that was driving her crazy. She just wanted to feel his hand on it, but he wasn't in any hurry, and she moaned.

The sound stopped the thrusting of his tongue, and his hand stilled. He removed it from under her top and broke the kiss.

"Alex, what—"

"Believe me, Amanda, I don't want to stop. But I don't want to do anything you're going to regret, either. Our daughters are inside, and they could come out at any minute."

How could she have forgotten? Even for a second?

"Don't feel guilty. We deserve to have some fun, too." There was amusement in his voice, and she knew he was thinking about their daughters' week at camp.

"Fun?" she asked, still feeling dazed by a passion she didn't understand.

"In very loose terms." Then he kissed her again, but it was restrained. And she knew if she just said the word, he'd arrange everything.

If and when she was ready.

Seven

Home from camp, Kristy and Heather quickly settled back into their routines. At the moment, the girls were having a powwow at the edge of Alex's property. He watched them from the back porch where he was reading the newspaper. Amanda was having dinner with another teacher from her building. They were going to shop for a wedding present for the first-grade teacher who was getting married. Immersed in an article about plans for a large shopping mall to be built in Cedar Grove, Alex didn't hear Kristy and Heather until they opened the door to the back porch.

"What's up, mates?" he teased, thinking they were going to ask him to go for ice cream.

"We want to tell you something," his daughter informed him. "It's *very* important."

The "very" caught his attention immediately. He closed and folded the newspaper and laid it on the glider beside him.

"I'm listening," he assured them.

Kristy looked a little nervous, which wasn't like her at all.

"What's wrong, honey?"

"Nothing's wrong. It's just . . . Well, I really, really miss having a mom. You're great, Dad. Honest, you are, but moms are . . . well, different . . . special. And I'd really, really like to have Mrs. Carson for my mom."

Alex couldn't say he was shocked. He knew how well Kristy and Amanda got along. He was just surprised Kristy was speaking so plainly about it. But then he looked at Heather. "And how would you feel about that?"

The nine-year-old smiled shyly. "I think it's a great idea. I've always wanted a sister. And I like you, Mr. Woodsides. I'd like having you for a dad."

Alex wasn't sure exactly what to say.

Kristy and Heather came closer to him and sat cross-legged on the floor in front of him. Kristy offered, "We just thought you should know, Dad, because you're the one who has to do the asking."

The asking. By that his daughter meant a marriage proposal. He supposed he would have come to that decision on his own in a little while, but the girls had made the idea more of a reality. "So you want me to ask Mrs. Carson to marry me?"

The two girls exchanged a look, then nodded. "We sure do," they said in unison.

Chuckling, he thought about how much brighter the world looked since Amanda had come into his life. "Let me think about it," he said with a smile.

Thinking about little else for the next two days, Alex finally decided the girls were right. Kristy needed a mom, Heather needed a dad, and he needed Amanda beside him in his bed every night. It would be very easy to combine their lives. All they had to do was sell her house. Knowing that Amanda had lost both her parents, that she had no living relatives, the idea of marriage sooner rather than later should make her happy.

After work, Alex picked up Kristy at his mother's, and then made another stop at a florist. Kristy was grinning from ear to ear as if she might suspect what he had planned. They drove to Amanda's house, both of them smiling at each other every few seconds. He'd called Amanda and told her not to cook dinner, that they'd take the girls to one of their favorite restaurants in Camp Hill, preferably one with great ice cream desserts. So he knew that she'd be waiting for them.

The front door was open, and he let Kristy proceed him inside. Amanda was paging through a magazine, while Heather sat on the floor across the room playing with a hand-held electronic game. When Kristy joined Heather on the floor, he crossed to where Amanda was sitting in the Boston rocker. She looked up at him, and he thought he'd never seen eyes as blue or as beautiful as hers. Presenting her with the bouquet of pink roses, he said, "I have something to ask you."

She took the flowers, rubbing her cheek against the rose petals, inhaling their fragrance, and responded, "Oh, Alex, they're beautiful. Thank you. With a surprise like these, you can ask me anything." There was laughter in her eyes, and he realized she had no idea what was coming.

Taking her hand, he drew her up before him.

Her laughter faded, and she searched his face. "What is it?"

After a quick glance at the girls, noticing their thumbs-up encouragement, he smiled. "Amanda Carson, will you marry me?"

Her mouth rounded with her slight gasp, and he decided some convincing wouldn't hurt. "Kristy wants you for a mother, and Heather tells me she'd like me for a dad. They both need two parents, and sooner rather than later."

Regaining some measure of composure, Amanda asked, "You've discussed this?" She was looking at the three of them.

"Yep, and it's unanimous. Except for your vote. What do you say?"

Her cheeks became pink. "Alex, this is so sudden. You expect me to give you an answer right this minute?"

Obviously she still wasn't convinced. He wasn't sure what to say or do, but it seemed wise to back off slightly . . . but only slightly. "I'll give you twenty-four hours to think about it. How's that?"

"Twenty-four hours?" she asked as if it were two minutes.

"Amanda, either we're right or we're wrong. I'm hoping you'll decide we're very right."

Both girls bobbed their heads.

After looking down at the flowers, Amanda looked back up at him. "All right. I'll give you my answer in twenty-four hours."

"I'll see if Mom can watch the girls tomorrow night. You can come over for dinner. Okay?"

"Okay," she agreed, still looking somewhat stunned.

He was feeling a little stunned himself. But tomorrow night could be the beginning of a new life for all of them.

Thunder rumbled in the distance, but Amanda was almost oblivious to it as she weeded her garden in an attempt to sort her thoughts. She hadn't slept last night. She'd closed her eyes. She'd plumped her pillow a thousand times. But all she could see was Alex's face. And all she could hear was his proposal and his reasons for making it—Kristy needed a mother and Heather needed a dad. Besides that, there was a smoldering desire in Alex's eyes that said he wanted her in his bed. Was all that enough for a good marriage? What about love?

Alex hadn't mentioned love.

She realized now that her attraction to Alex was much more than attraction. Yes, she felt as if she'd go up in flames when he looked at her or touched her or kissed her. But she admired him as a man, his ability to love his daughter, his tenderness, his strength of character. She'd fallen deeply in love with him. But did he love her? Wanting a life with her wasn't the same as loving her, was it?

Maybe it was. Maybe he couldn't put his feelings into words. Maybe his desire was his way of showing her his feelings. He'd told her he wanted her to be ready, and maybe he'd realized they wouldn't be ready until they made a commitment to each other and a commitment to a life together. Maybe he knew her better than she knew herself.

Amanda had married Jeff when she wasn't mature enough or experienced enough to realize what a marriage needed, how it had to be nurtured, the emotional investment both people had to make. With Alex . . . they could laugh and play and talk. She felt Alex needed her in some way he didn't want to admit, just as she needed him and didn't want to admit it. They could be independent, yet together, as well as respect each other as equals. That was a very special gift only Alex could give her, and she could give him.

The back screen door slammed, and Heather came running to Amanda. "You'd better come in, Mom. It's gonna rain."

Amanda laughed. "Do you think I'm going to melt if I get wet?"

Heather wrinkled her nose. "Aw, Mom, you know what I mean. Besides, it's almost time for you to get ready. You don't want to be late."

Although her daughter hadn't said as much, Amanda realized that Heather was as excited as she was about tonight.

"Did you decide on your answer yet?" Heather asked.

The wind picked up as more black clouds gathered, and Amanda rose to her feet. "Yes, I have. If you're sure you approve, I'm going to tell Alex I want to marry him."

Heather let out a yelp and hugged her mother tight around the waist. Amanda hugged her back, sure she was making the right decision, sure that as soon as Alex could feel the depth and breadth of her love for him, he could tell her he loved her, too.

The storm that had threatened all afternoon let loose that evening. Alex had just returned from taking Kristy and Heather to his parents' house and was setting up the dining room for dinner with Amanda when rain poured from the sky in torrents. He was spreading the white tablecloth that he'd borrowed from his mother on his dining room table when the first flash of lightning ricocheted across the sky. The humidity, along with the high temperature, had been unbearable all day. For most of the afternoon he'd cleaned out and made necessary repairs on his storage shed. The truth was he was too restless to do anything else—and worried. What if Amanda didn't accept his proposal?

When he'd picked up Heather, Amanda had waved from the door and he'd wanted to kidnap her right then and there and make her say yes. But he knew he had to wait. He knew he had to set the atmosphere. He knew he had to do everything just right.

The problem was—he needed to get a shower, and the lightning wasn't going to stop him. He'd be in and out in five minutes. Then he could finish setting up downstairs. He'd ordered dinner from the best restaurant in town and paid to have it delivered between seven and seven-thirty. By seven-thirty, when Amanda was due to arrive, everything would be perfect.

His first indication that perfection was going to be a little difficult to achieve came when he was showering. The thunder clapped so loud it felt as if it were in the house. No sooner had the boom sounded than the light in the bathroom went off, followed by another boom. Hoping the storm had simply tripped the circuit breakers, Alex quickly finished, turned off the spigot, and toweled off. But when he went into the bedroom to dress, none of the lights would go on, and he guessed the electricity was out. That wouldn't be so bad. They could eat by candlelight. But the humidity was still high, and it wouldn't be long until the inside of the house felt like a rain forest.

Quickly stepping into a pair of khaki shorts, he went down to the basement to check the breakers. But after checking the box, he knew the electricity was definitely out, and that meant not only the lights but the air conditioning. He'd just have to open the windows as far as he could so that the rain didn't pour in and hope the breeze would keep the house below oven temperature. But as he set the dining room table, rain pelted in the window, wetting the windowsill, and he slammed the sash down with an oath, going to the kitchen for a towel to mop up the mess.

At seven o'clock, his doorbell rang. Alex had just finished mopping up other windowsills and setting the table and still hadn't dressed. When he went to the door, he found Amanda standing under an umbrella, her flowered silk blouse and short skirt molding to her in the damp weather and breeze. Her gaze passed from his bare shoulders down the middle of his chest to the band on his shorts . . . If he hadn't been feeling the lack of air conditioning before, he was now.

Quickly lifting her gaze to his face again, her cheeks pinkened, and she motioned to her car in his driveway. "I drove because of the weather."

When he opened the screen door for her, she closed her umbrella and propped it next to the door. As she stepped over the threshold, her arm brushed his chest, and they both seemed to hold their breath.

Letting the door close, he said, "You're early."

"I thought I could help." Her smile was apologetic.

Uh-oh! She thought *he* was cooking dinner. "Uh . . . I'm still getting ready, and . . . I don't want to disappoint you, but dinner is being catered."

At that moment a mini-van pulled into his driveway and parked behind Amanda's car. In the torrential rain, the driver hopped out, went around to the sliding door, opened it and took out a stack of styrofoam containers. Then he ran up to the door, a piece of paper in his hand—which he shoved at Alex.

Alex let the man inside and watched him drip all

over his foyer. The receipt was soaked, and beads of water fell from the styrofoam. Pulling money from his pocket, Alex shoved it into the man's hand and took the containers from him saying, "Keep the change."

"Lousy night, ain't it?" the man asked. The bill from his baseball cap dripped water onto the money as he counted it.

Amanda laid her purse on the marble-topped foyer table. "That depends on how you spend the night," she said with a smile. "I'll get some towels," she added and then went into the kitchen.

Alex knew Amanda had a good sense of humor. He just wasn't sure how good it would be with his plans for tonight derailing one by one. After the delivery man left, a fine mist sprayed in the screen door, and Alex had to shut the main door with his foot. So much for letting a breeze in.

Carrying dinner to the kitchen, noticing at least the containers were still warm, he deposited them on the counter. "I hope you like chicken cordon bleu because . . ." But when he lifted the lid, he made a face. The smell of onions hit him first, and then the aroma of liver. Suspecting that take-out dinners had been mistakenly switched, he swore long and hard. When he faced Amanda, she looked . . . not shocked, not surprised, just very concerned.

Laying the towels she had found on the counter, she asked gently, "Alex, what's wrong?"

He blew out a long breath. "I wanted tonight to be right . . . special." He might as well not even mention perfect. "Not something out of a sitcom."

Coming over beside him, she peeked into the container. "You don't like liver and onions, I take it?" Her wrist brushed his arm, her soft skin sliding across his, intensifying the heat already in the kitchen.

"Do *you?*" he murmured.

Turning toward him, her bangs curling in the humidity, her hair waving more than usual around her face, she looked up at him with honest, wide blue eyes. "Not particularly. Why don't we see what else we have?"

But he couldn't remember what else he'd ordered, let alone care about it. Her perfume wound around him, the silkiness of her outfit invited his touch, her pretty pink lips mesmerized him. He hadn't even had time to finish dressing. The night was turning into a disaster, and if he didn't kiss her right now . . .

His hand slid into her hair as his lips met hers. He loved the feel of it; he loved the feel of her. Her silk blouse caught against his chest and moved as he did, sliding over her breasts, making him crazy with needing her. Even before his tongue entered her mouth, he wanted anything and everything she could give him. But he couldn't take it, not yet, not until he knew her answer.

Hotter than he'd ever been in his life from both the end-of-July heat and the fiery desire inside him, he broke away and swore again. "I promised myself I wasn't going to push you, that I wasn't going to ask before dinner. But for God's sake, Amanda . . ."

The passion they'd stirred up was alive on her face and in her eyes, and suddenly he could see she knew the power she had over him. And she was going to use it.

With a slow sensual smile, her voice sexy and low, she came as close to him as she possibly could. "We can still make this evening as special as we want it. And

I think since you've gone to so much trouble, we can improvise a little."

"Improvise what? It's so damned hot in here," he muttered.

She laughed, and the sound of it swept through him like music he'd needed all his life. "I think it's going to get dark sooner rather than later. Why don't we put together whatever dinner we can and take it onto the porch?" she suggested. "We can have a picnic on the floor, and light some citronella candles."

Alex was beginning to get the idea, and he liked it even better than his. But as far as her giving him an answer—"You're going to make me wait, aren't you?"

"The anticipation might be worth the wait," she answered coyly.

Geez. Getting through dinner was going to require forbearance. And he didn't know what they were going to eat. Tipping her chin up, he thought, *two can play this game.* Slowly he traced his finger back and forth across her lips. "I hope you have a magic wand in your pocket, or we might starve."

Playing the game with him, her tongue came out and teased his finger. Then she nipped the tip and turned back toward the counter, setting aside the liver and onions and opening the other containers. One held broccoli and cauliflower layered with cheese, another braised new potatoes. The last box contained large red fresh strawberries and a cup of whipped cream.

"This is going to be easy," she said, going toward the refrigerator. "I know you have eggs, so all I need is a frying pan. It's a good thing you have a gas stove."

In amazement, Alex watched Amanda transform a disaster into something very special.

While she worked at the stove, he mopped up the water in the foyer, then went upstairs and pulled out of the closet the down comforter he used in the winter. He also gathered a few pillows. Fortunately, the rain had mostly blown in on the front side of the house and the porch was dry. After he passed through the kitchen and gave Amanda a wink, he spread out the comforter and the pillows on top of the carpet. Taking the cushions from the furniture out there, he added those to the mix. Then he lit the citronella candles. Lowering the roll-up blinds on two sides of the porch, he realized this would be as private as inside the house. Yet the wind, which had died down to a breeze, gently filtered through the screens, filling the porch with the scent of the now gentle rain.

When Alex returned to the kitchen, he found Amanda had fixed two plates—fluffy omelets filled with the broccoli, cheese and cauliflower accompanied by the potatoes. She'd mounded the strawberries into a bowl. After they carried their dinner to the back porch and settled on the floor, he poured two glasses of wine. At least that was chilled. He'd stuck it in the refrigerator last night.

And he had the small velvet box in his pocket.

After he'd dropped off the girls, he'd stopped at a jewelry store. He'd told himself maybe he was being premature, that maybe Amanda's answer wouldn't be what he hoped. But he'd bought the marquise-cut diamond anyway.

They took a sip of their wine, ate, smiled at each other, and now and then talked about something insignificant. The buildup was tremendous, a sort of foreplay in itself. Alex watched each forkful of food disappear into Amanda's mouth. She was a sensual eater, just as she was a sensual kisser, and he wondered if she even knew it. By the time he sated his hunger for food, he was more than ready to satisfy another appetite. And he didn't think he could prolong the suspense any longer.

Pouring more wine into both of their glasses, he lifted his. "We didn't toast."

She lifted her glass, too. "What should we toast to?"

He said, "You tell me."

Unfolding her legs, she moved closer to him until her glass almost met his. "I think we should toast our upcoming marriage. I want to be your wife, Alex. My answer is yes."

Toasts forgotten, he took her glass from her and set it with his on a table out of the way. "I think we should save dessert for later," he murmured.

But Amanda just smiled at him as she had in the kitchen, lifted a strawberry from the top of the bowl and dipped it into the whipped cream. Then she offered it to him. "Maybe we should have just one."

He was aroused without her touching him, and when she lifted the strawberry to his mouth, he took a bite, held it in his teeth, and then leaned over to her. She took it from him, their lips brushing only slightly. They watched each other as they finished their pieces, and then he brought his lips to hers. She tasted of strawberries and whipped cream and woman. His heart pounded so loud he couldn't think. He only wanted to feel her surround him. As her hands explored his chest, he groaned, and when her fingertips brushed his nipples, he took her down onto the pillows and covered her with his body.

Breaking the kiss, he said in a hoarse voice, "I want this to be perfect for you. But I need you so much . . ."

She slid her hand from his shoulder into the hair at the nape of his neck. "It *will* be perfect, because I need you, too."

Nothing in the world could have stopped Alex then. He was going to make her his in every sense of the word. Unfastening the buttons of her blouse, he hurried to brush it aside. The lace bra was the color of peach champagne, almost the color of her skin. After he unfastened it, he cupped her breasts in his palms and watched her eyes grow wide with passion, as his fingertips slid over the nipples. "Do you know how many times I've dreamed of doing this?"

She shook her head, then reached out and unfastened the button on his shorts. "Do you know how many times I've dreamed of doing this?"

With a deep laugh that was almost a groan, he got rid of his shorts and briefs, then stripped her skirt and panties from her. When he laid her back on the pillows again, he slid down her body until he was kissing the hollow at her neck, the swell of her breasts, the indentation of her navel. She writhed sensually under him, and he didn't know how long he could last. When he touched her intimately, her pleasure was evident.

"Are you ready for me?" he asked.

Amanda gazed at him with such tenderness, he thought he'd die. "Yes."

He intended to take it slow, he intended to be gentle. But at the first touch of her velvet heat, he couldn't hold back, and he thrust into her with a groan. She wrapped her legs around him and rocked with him in rhythm with the night and the rain and passion they'd denied themselves for weeks. Alex's thrusts became long and deep and hard until she cried out, calling his name, clasping his shoulders in cadence with the waves of pleasure sweeping over her.

The sound of his name on her lips catapulted him over the edge, bringing him a release so sweet and euphoric that he lost track of place and time. There was only Amanda and the ecstasy they'd shared.

And when he rolled to his side and tenderly caressed her face, he saw tears in her eyes. "Amanda, are you okay? I didn't mean for it to happen so fast—"

Reaching out, she stroked his jaw. "It wasn't fast, Alex. It was perfect . . . so perfect."

After he kissed her again, he grabbed his shorts and rummaged in the pocket. Then he brought out the velvet box and held it out to her.

She opened it, and her eyes filled up again. "It's beautiful," she whispered.

He took the ring from the box and slid it onto her finger. It fit perfectly. Then he kissed her again. Finally pulling away, he said, "Amanda, I didn't even think about protection. But I want more children. Do you?"

She nodded. "I'd love more children."

With a grin, he suggested, "Then let's get married as soon as possible."

Eight

Laughter drifted into the kitchen from the back yard on Monday evening, and Amanda went to her door and looked out. Alex was playing croquet with Heather and Kristy. The sight of the three of them together made Amanda smile, and she went back to the stove and switched off the pot of corn-on-the-cob that she was fixing.

Saturday night had been so special. Making love with Alex . . . She just never thought she could feel like that about a man, or love so deeply. Yesterday they'd spent the entire day with the girls, planning, making calls to find a minister who would marry them. They were getting married in two weeks in Alex's back yard, and there was so much to do. A real estate agent was coming over tonight to appraise her house before they put it on the market. Everything was moving so fast, and yet it all felt so right.

When the phone rang, Amanda picked it up, gazing down at her engagement ring, still feeling as if she were dreaming.

"Amanda, is that you? It's Jeff."

Jeff? Her ex-husband? For a moment her heart tripped, and then she told herself there was nothing to be anxious about. They were no longer married.

He didn't have control over her any longer. "Jeff, this is a surprise. How did you find me?"

"I asked around and found out you'd taken a job in Cedar Grove. You're listed, Amanda. It wasn't hard."

Just as he always had, he was making her feel inferior. Well, she wouldn't feel inferior—not any more. "What do you want, Jeff?"

She thought she heard him sigh. "Look, Amanda, I'd like to see you. Could we have lunch or something one day this week?"

"Are you in Cedar Grove?"

"No. But I'll drive over if that's what you want. I took a few days off."

Days off? Jeff had never taken vacations. As head of the new products division of a company that made medical equipment, he had often worked until midnight. But she supposed he could have changed in three years. "Can you tell me what this is about?"

"I'd rather wait until I see you."

She was almost afraid to ask her next question, but she did anyway. "Do you want me to bring Heather?"

"No. I just need to talk to you about something. When can we meet?"

Thinking it was best to get it over with, she said, "How about tomorrow?"

"That's fine. Where do you want me to meet you?"

Cedar Grove wasn't that big, nor were there many choices. For a moment, she thought about meeting him in Camp Hill, but she didn't have anything to hide. Choosing the restaurant about a block from the school, she told him its name and gave him directions. "If you see the elementary school, you've gone too far."

"I'll find it."

"Around one?" she asked. "Any lunch crowd should be thinning out by then."

"One's good. I'll see you tomorrow. Thanks, Amanda."

After she said good-bye, she hung up. The Jeff she'd known wouldn't have thanked her. The Jeff she'd known wouldn't have let her set the day or time. But if he needed something from her . . .

What could her ex-husband possibly want?

The heat was unbearable in Amanda's house, and after the real estate agent left, Alex suggested they all spend the night in the air conditioning at his house. Amanda told Alex she would sleep in one of his guest bedrooms. After all, they had two daughters to set an example for now. He gave her a patient smile, but she suspected from the gleam in his eyes that either he wasn't going to be staying in his room for the whole night or she wouldn't be staying in hers. During supper and their meeting with the real estate agent, she couldn't help but think about her phone conversation with Jeff. She should tell Alex about it, and yet . . .

She remembered how he had been jealous of Ted Livingston. With the wedding two weeks away she didn't want to upset him. So she rationalized that there was no point telling him about her lunch until she found out what Jeff wanted.

After they gathered a few things and went to Alex's house, they put the girls to bed in Kristy's room. Alex leaned close to her and whispered in her ear, "I bought some more strawberries. We could sit on the back porch and feed them to each other."

"Oh?" she said flirtatiously.

He wrapped his arm around her waist. "Yep. And neck a little bit. Then maybe I can convince you to sneak into my bedroom for the night."

She laughed. "You think strawberries are going to do that?"

"Nope. But the necking might." He pulled her to him and stole a quick kiss. Draping his arm around her shoulders, they went down the stairs together.

In the kitchen, he crossed to the refrigerator and pulled out the bowl of strawberries. But instead of teasing her further, he set them on the counter. "Is anything wrong, Amanda?"

"No. Why?"

"You seem preoccupied tonight. Are you having second thoughts?"

The worry in his eyes made her feel a little guilty for not telling him about Jeff. Yet her desire not to argue about anything before the wedding made her say only, "There's just a lot to think about. Selling the house and moving is a bit unsettling, let alone planning a menu for the caterer, finding music for the wedding and reception, looking for a wedding dress . . ."

When she trailed off, he curled his arm around her and tugged her close. "I get the idea."

With their bodies pressed together, she realized he had other ideas, too, and she smiled. He lowered his head and kissed her neck. Then he moved to her earlobe and flicked it with his tongue.

"Alex," she said breathlessly.

"What?" he murmured, returning to her neck, then kissing her shoulder.

When he nudged her tank top and bra strap aside,

she managed, "We can't do this in the kitchen. Not with the girls here."

"We'll never make it to the bedroom," he breathed right before his lips captured hers. His tongue dashed inside her mouth and she returned his fervor. No, they wouldn't make it to the bedroom, but they certainly couldn't make love here . . .

Obviously thinking the same thing, Alex kept kissing her, but drew her with him out onto the porch. Then he locked the door to the house and closed it behind them. On the porch, the humid night air surrounded them, and they couldn't take off their clothes fast enough. It was pitch black, and they couldn't see, only feel. Alex didn't even attempt to turn on a light. He kissed her as he took her down to the floor. His mouth was wet and hot on her breasts and her stomach, and he kept going down further until she clutched his shoulders. "Alex . . ."

"I want to kiss you everywhere, Amanda. Everywhere."

And he did until she thought she'd go out of her mind with needing him. His lips on her inner thighs made her arch up. His tongue on the center of her pleasure began a wave of ecstasy that intensified as he thrust into her again and again and again. She couldn't imagine needing him more or loving him more, and when the climax came, she embraced it as she embraced him, forgetting about tomorrow and living for the moment, hoping for a lifetime of moments with Alex.

Only three tables were filled at the Blue Door Family Restaurant when Amanda went inside. She spotted

Jeff immediately in the back corner at a table. Standing when she came toward him, he waited for her to be seated. He looked the same, his light-brown hair trimmed short in an executive cut, his lean physique not any heavier. He was wearing a short-sleeved shirt open at the neck and brown casual slacks. The sight of him stirred anxiety inside of her but nothing else.

They stared at each other awkwardly for a few moments until he said, "I thought you might not show up."

She folded her hands in her lap and told him the truth. "I considered doing just that, but it didn't seem like a good idea. After all, as you said, I'm listed." Though soon she'd be listed under a different name, she thought happily.

"Amanda, my life's changing and I'm trying to change with it." The man who had always shown her a self-assured front suddenly looked uncomfortable. Not explaining further, he simply looked at her engagement ring. "It looks as if you're going to be getting married."

"In two weeks," she told him, but decided she didn't have to give him any of the details.

The waitress, a young woman who looked to be in her twenties, came over to take their orders then. Quickly looking at the menu, they both decided on club sandwiches and iced tea.

When she was out of earshot, Jeff said, "I'm moving to Texas."

"Texas?"

"The company is opening a new office in Houston, and Nancy and I decided we needed a change—" He stopped abruptly. "That's not true. Our marriage was on the rocks, and we're trying to put it back together. I couldn't . . . fail a second time."

He looked as if the word "fail" was very difficult for him to say, and she couldn't imagine him using it. The old Jeff would never have said he was anything but successful. Time and time again she had asked him to go to counseling with her, and he wouldn't. Amanda wasn't sure what to say now, but finally responded, "Two people have to work on a marriage."

"I guess I've finally learned that—the hard way. Nancy moved out for a while, then I found out that she was pregnant and didn't tell me. That was almost as bad as when I found out that you wanted a divorce." The silence between them was filled with past hurts, not simply memories.

Softly Amanda asked, "Why did you want to see me?"

After a pause, Jeff answered, "Because I'm trying to clean up my past. I'm trying to make some things right—" Again he stopped and didn't look as if he knew how to put it. "I was a coward to turn my back on you and Heather. You'd hurt me, so I cut you both out of my life."

"Heather never hurt you."

He met Amanda's gaze squarely. "I know that now. But back then, you were both the same package. She doesn't know me, and she probably doesn't want to know me, and I'm not going to pretend I can be a father if I'm in Texas and she's here." He looked again at Amanda's right hand. "And from the way it looks, she's going to have a new father."

"Yes, she is."

"Does he like kids?"

"He loves them. He has one of his own."

Jeff looked troubled. "I never knew how to act around kids, but I guess I'm going to have to learn. The thing is, and part of this is still selfish, I don't want Heather to hate me."

Amanda had tried very hard not to be bitter, not to let disappointment with Jeff and their marriage touch their daughter. "She doesn't hate you, Jeff."

"As she gets older, she's going to think about things. It could come to that. The reason I asked you here is I want to set up a college fund for her. I could put it in her name and turn it over to her when she's eighteen, but I thought it would be better if you knew about it, if she knew about it. She can watch it grow that way. And maybe she won't think so badly of me."

If Jeff gave Heather money, he'd probably want to control it. He might even want to choose her college. Should she even think about having contact with him again? Should she let him salve his uneasy conscience by giving their daughter money?

"I know this is something you have to think about, especially if you're getting married again. And if you want me to forget about the whole idea, I will. But I'd really like to do this, Amanda. I feel I need to do this."

The waitress brought their order and set their sandwiches and drinks in front of them. Then she tilted her head and smiled at Amanda. "When I took your order, I thought I recognized you. Aren't you the third grade teacher at Cedar Grove Elementary?"

Distracted by what Jeff had offered, Amanda tried her best to give her attention to the waitress and nodded, "Yes, I am."

"You'll have my daughter in the fall. My aunt, Clara Webb, pointed you out to me at the carnival. You know, when you were stuck up on top of the Ferris wheel?"

Amanda remembered that night very well. It was the first time Alex had kissed her. "Clara didn't tell me I'd be having her niece this year. I'll be in school at least a week before it starts to prepare my classroom. Make sure you stop in with your daughter and say hi. We'll get acquainted early."

The young woman smiled again. "We'll be sure to do that. Enjoy your lunch." Then she went to wait on two customers who had seated themselves shortly before.

Spreading her napkin on her lap, Amanda looked back at Jeff, still absorbing all the things he'd told her. "I'll think about your offer."

He took a business card out of his pocket and handed it to her. "Both my home and office numbers are on there. We won't be leaving until September. Don't be afraid to call me at home. Nancy knows I'm here today, and she understands this is something I have to do."

Amanda picked up a quarter of her sandwich. If she told Alex about this, she was pretty sure he'd tell her to forget about her ex-husband's money. But there was more involved here than money. She was going to think about this very carefully, and make the decision on her own.

On Wednesday afternoon, Alex sat at his desk, shuffling through travel brochures. He'd gone to a travel agency over lunch and discussed possibilities for a honeymoon. There was a resort on a lake in Vermont that had a honeymoon suite open for the week after their wedding, as well as a bed-and-breakfast in Maine on a bluff overlooking the ocean. Those were his favorites. But he'd show everything to Amanda and let her pick out what she liked best. He was amazed at how much she'd accomplished so quickly.

Last night she'd gone shopping with his mother, and both had been secretive about what they were wearing for the wedding. He smiled. That was all part of the fun. After the shopping trip, his mother had stayed with Kristy and Heather for a while, and he and Amanda escaped to her house for a quick tryst. If their lovemaking was only half this exciting for the rest of their marriage, he'd be a very happy man. Still . . .

Something seemed to be bothering Amanda. He couldn't quite put his finger on it, and he hoped it was simply pre-wedding jitters. Perhaps he *had* rushed her into this.

When his intercom buzzed, he picked up the phone. Georgia said to him, "It's a Mrs. Webb."

Alex ran his hand through his hair and sighed. She probably wanted to know when their next meeting was going to be. Looking at his calendar, he decided it could wait until the week after his honeymoon.

Taking Mrs. Webb off hold, he said, "Hello, Clara. How can I help you?"

"Just checking to see how our speaker list is growing."

"Twenty-one, so far. I'm going to make a few calls and pull in some favors. We'll get our thirty."

"You certainly know how to get things done, Alex." Hardly pausing for a breath, she went on, "By the way, my niece said she waited on Amanda yesterday at the Blue Door Restaurant."

Amanda hadn't mentioned that she'd had lunch out, but she had so many errands to run for the wedding, he wasn't surprised. Kristy had asked him if she could stay with Amanda and Heather during the day. "That's the way it's going to be after the wedding anyway," were his daughter's exact words. His mother had understood, and since she was in the process of packing up for her move to Florida, it seemed to be the best arrangement for everyone. But she'd told both him and Amanda she'd keep the girls any time they were particularly busy.

"Amanda probably thought Kristy and Heather deserved a lunch out after running errands all morning for the wedding."

"Oh, but the girls weren't with her! Some man was."

Clara Webb was not one of Alex's favorite people, and he didn't want to encourage her gossiping. But he suddenly wanted to know everything she knew.

Clara chattered on. "I didn't see them myself. My niece waited on them, and she said he was good-looking but that he had light brown hair. That's how I knew it wasn't you."

Light brown. That wasn't Ted; he was unmistakably blond. Just who did Amanda have lunch with, and why hadn't she told him about it? He remembered not so long ago Heather saying that Amanda went out every weekend. What about those men she'd dated? Did she still have feelings for any of them? He'd courted her so quickly. He thought they'd both been caught up in the whirlwind of finding each other . . .

"I remember now, Clara. I think she was meeting him to discuss music for the wedding. Something like that."

"Oh, I see," Clara responded, sounding disappointed. "Well, I guess I won't keep you any longer. Just let me know when our next meeting is."

A meeting for Career Day was the last thing on

Alex's mind right now. Confronting Amanda about her lunch date was first.

When Alex arrived home that evening, Amanda had just put supper on his dining room table. The girls were already seated. His last appointment had run late. Usually he called Amanda when he was going to be late, but today he knew his voice would give something away if he talked to her. He had to see her face when he asked her what she'd done for lunch yesterday.

"We were afraid you weren't going to make it," she said.

Unbuttoning his shirt cuffs, he rolled up his sleeves. "Lots of complications today," he said vaguely. All afternoon he'd told himself not to jump to conclusions. All afternoon he'd told himself Amanda wouldn't lie to him. All afternoon he'd tried to tamp down the anger that had continued to build.

The girls chattered about their day—going to the florist and looking at all sorts of flowers, visiting the bakery and seeing many shapes and sizes of wedding cakes.

Amanda jumped in then. "I brought home a book with pictures of wedding cakes. That way we can decide what we want, and you won't have to go into the bakery."

She looked so happy, so innocent, it was hard for him to believe she was keeping something from him.

And just in case his conversation with Clara Webb hadn't been sheer fabrication on his part, he asked his fiancée, "Did you find anyone for the music yet?"

"I put in a few calls, but I'm waiting for everyone to call me back."

He took another shot, knowing it was a very long shot. "How about the photographer?"

"We're meeting with him next week at his studio. Monday was the earliest he could fit us in. I hope Monday night's okay with you."

"It's fine," he murmured, knowing that nothing was fine, but that he had to wait until they were alone to have his questions answered.

After Amanda served a lemon cake she had made, the girls asked if they could go outside and play in the lean-to.

"Stay away from the creek," Alex warned. "With all the rain we've had, it's high."

"We will," they chorused and left the dining room, eager to play outside for as long as daylight allowed.

As Amanda began to clear the table, she glanced at Alex cautiously. "Rough day?"

Alex hadn't kissed her when he'd come home, and he knew she was probably wondering why. There was no easy way to do this, so he'd might as well get it over with the fastest way possible. "What did you do for lunch yesterday?"

She paled and set the dishes she'd picked up back down on the table. "That sounds like an accusation." Her shoulders straightened and her blue eyes sparked with silver.

"It's only an accusation if you're guilty of something."

"Guilty? Because I went out to lunch?"

"Clara Webb told me her niece saw you with a man. Where were the girls and who was the man, Amanda?"

As soon as he asked, he could tell by her demeanor

that he was going about this all wrong, but he didn't know how else to do it.

"Debbie was with the girls. Don't you trust me, Alex?"

"Look, Amanda, I know you dated lots of men before I came along. Heather told me. We haven't been together that long, and if you still have feelings for any of them—"

"Feelings?" She was angry now, too. "I don't know what you're talking about. I didn't date *any* men before you came along."

"You dated Ted Livingston."

"That was *after* you came along, and it was one date, the only date, I might add, that I'd had since my divorce."

Alex wanted to believe her. He really did. "Why would Heather tell me you went out every weekend?"

After a pensive silence, she didn't answer him but asked, "Did *you* date?"

"No." He felt foolish admitting it, but he'd always been honest with her. "You were the first woman I wanted to go out with."

Amanda came around the table to where he was standing. "Kristy told me differently the first Saturday night after I started keeping her."

"The only thing I do on Saturday nights is go to the grocery store. Heather told me you like to get dressed up and wear lipstick and go out almost every weekend."

Amanda shook her head. "I do—to church every Sunday morning."

Fixing his gaze on her, realizing she'd detoured from his question, he asked, "Why would they lie?"

"I think our two daughters have been matchmaking. I'm not sure Kristy ever had a real problem with math. She just wanted me to tutor her so we'd get together."

"You mean we were set up?" he growled.

Hurt shadowed Amanda's face. "Don't you like the result?"

Tension vibrated between them until he asked again, "Who was the man, Amanda?"

Her voice low, she answered, "It was Jeff, my ex-husband. He called and asked if he could meet me. He's going through some kind of . . . life change. He almost lost his wife, and he's realized he treated me and Heather badly. He's offered to set up a college fund for her." She said it all in a rush as if that could somehow minimize its impact.

But Alex couldn't believe Amanda's ex-husband had called, and she hadn't told him about it. He couldn't believe she had met the man and had lunch and hadn't told him about that, either. This offer of money for Heather could affect both of their lives. "You refused him, of course," Alex said, his voice filled with anger.

She met his gaze unflinchingly. "I haven't decided yet."

Alex's gut clenched. "I see. You didn't think I needed to know your ex-husband called. You didn't think I needed to know you were meeting him for lunch. And apparently you don't think I have any say in this decision. I see very clearly, Amanda."

"Alex . . ."

He raked his hand through his hair, feeling betrayed by her in some deep elemental way, so betrayed he didn't want to deal with it. "The first thing we'd better do is talk to the girls about their lies and maneuvering." His voice carried the remoteness he used to distance himself from his emotions.

After a few moments in which Amanda looked as if she wanted to contradict him, she capitulated. "All right. I'll go get them." But she looked upset as she crossed the kitchen and went through the screened-in porch.

He went to the living room and paced . . . and waited.

A few minutes later, Amanda brought the girls inside, and they sat on the sofa with a perplexed look on their faces. "What's wrong, Dad?" Kristy asked. "You don't look so happy."

"That's because I don't think you've been honest with me, or with Amanda." His gaze rested on Heather. "Or you, either. Heather, didn't you tell me your mother went out every weekend?"

Heather bowed her head and looked down at her lap. "Yes."

"Was that the truth?"

When she looked up at him again, she answered, "Well, sort of. She does go out every weekend. She goes to church."

"But you knew I would think she was going out on dates?"

Amanda's daughter nodded.

"And Kristy, you told Amanda I was going out?"

His daughter straightened up defensively. "You were. You were going for groceries."

"Kristy!" His exasperation was clear and both girls hung their heads.

"And then there's your math grades," Alex continued, his gaze fixed on his daughter. "Did you let them slip on purpose?"

This time when Kristy looked up at him, her eyes glistened with tears. "Dad, please don't be mad. I wanted a mom so bad, and Mrs. Carson was just great. And Heather needs a dad, and we wanted to be sisters!"

Only then did Alex look at Amanda.

"They were only trying to arrange everybody's happiness," she murmured.

"Well you can't expect to be happy when you lie, and when you mislead other people." His look at her was pointed.

After a few moments of quiet that seemed to last a year, Amanda said, "Heather, go collect your things. We're not going to stay here tonight."

"But, Mom . . ."

And at the same time, Kristy wailed, "But, Dad . . ."

"We're not happy with what you girls did," Alex said. "But there are some other problems, too, that we have to think about. We've been spending a lot of time together, and tonight it's just a good idea not to. Do you want me to drive you home?" he asked Amanda.

"We don't have that much. We can walk. But I'll clean up supper first."

"You don't have to. And for now, I'll take Kristy to my mother's while I'm working. I think that'll be best."

The tension between them was so great he couldn't stand to stay in the living room or to look at Amanda and wonder what else she hadn't told him or what else she might not tell him in the future. He went into the kitchen. Something was very wrong, and he had no idea what to do about it.

Nine

Heartsick about what had happened with Alex last night, Amanda picked up the phone around ten a.m. the next morning and dialed his office. But his secretary informed her that he was meeting with a client and couldn't be disturbed. Amanda left a message. When he hadn't called back by three in the afternoon, she called a second time, but again he was supposedly involved in a meeting. It was possible, yet it was also likely he was avoiding her calls.

Around supper time, she tried Alex at home, but his answering machine clicked on. Besides her own heartache, she was worried about Heather, who thought Amanda's distress stemmed from her and Kristy's matchmaking efforts. Amanda had tried to convince her daughter that she and Alex had had a disagreement about something else, too. But she imagined Kristy was feeling as badly as Heather. She wanted to talk to Alex about that as well. She'd tucked Heather in for the night and was wondering if she should try to reach Alex at his mother's when her phone rang.

Snatching it up before it could ring a second time, she said, "Hello."

"It's Alex, Amanda. One appointment bumped into another all day, and I couldn't return your calls."

"I was hoping you could come over."

"It's late. We just got home, and Kristy is getting ready for bed."

"Heather isn't asleep yet. We could come up to your place."

There was a long pause, and then Alex responded, "It's been a long day, Amanda."

"For me, too, but we can't resolve anything if we don't talk. Heather was upset today. She thinks you're angry with her, and that's why you and I—" She couldn't seem to find the right words.

"Mom said Kristy moped around all day, too. And to be honest, I don't know what to tell her." He was silent for a few moments. "I'll pick you up tomorrow night. We can take the girls over to Mom's, and you and I can go somewhere and talk."

"Alex, I . . ." She wanted to tell him she loved him, but she was afraid he wouldn't believe her. She was afraid all he'd ever wanted was a mother for Kristy. "I'll see you tomorrow night, then."

His good night didn't carry any warmth, and she felt as if he'd put up walls all around himself. But she couldn't forget that he hadn't trusted her, that he'd thought she was seeing another man behind his back.

But if he could believe that, then he didn't know her at all.

When Alex picked up Amanda and Heather on Friday evening, the atmosphere in the car was anything but light. He smiled at Heather, and Amanda smiled at Kristy, but it didn't do much good. The two girls still looked as if they'd lost their best friend. After he dropped their daughters at his mother's, he drove toward the edge of town to the baseball field. There was a game in progress, but Alex parked a good distance from the other cars and pointed to the benches placed here and there along the creek. "We can go over there and have some privacy," he said.

Amanda was aware that he had chosen neutral territory.

Coming around to her side of the car, he opened her door, but his gaze gave nothing away. She couldn't tell what he was feeling, if he was feeling anything. As they walked toward one of the benches, tall grass tickled her legs, and she knew any other time she'd love being here with Alex. But tonight . . .

He waited until she'd seated herself on the bench, and then he positioned himself a good foot away. He was giving her plenty of signals that she needed to make the first move.

"There are a lot of reasons why I didn't tell you I was meeting Jeff."

Alex gave her a quick glance, then stared back at the creek.

Hoping she could make him understand, she plowed in. "When I was married, I tried to do everything in my power to please Jeff. But I never could. He was always critical of something, whether it was the way I made dinner, or the way I dressed, or how I kept the house. When he started to work longer and longer hours, I thought it was my fault and that he just didn't want to come home to me, or Heather. I asked him to go to counseling with me lots of times, but he never would."

When Alex made no comment, she went on. "I wanted a family so badly, and I wanted to believe in marriage. But Jeff tried to control everything I did.

He wanted an accounting of every minute I wasn't with him, of everything I did with Heather, of every penny I spent. I was suffocating, feeling like a prisoner. I went back to teaching when Heather was three, and we had a terrible argument about it. He wanted me to stay at home, but I needed to be around other people. And I needed to have something of my own. I found a wonderful day-care provider for Heather, and at least when I was teaching, I felt free. I desperately wanted our marriage to succeed. But then I found out he was having an affair."

The nerve in Alex's jaw worked, and she could see he wasn't unaffected by what she'd said, but still he didn't look at her. "Alex, please try and understand. When I got a divorce, I promised myself I would never let anyone make decisions for me again, or treat me as if I were inferior. My main goal was to teach Heather how to be an independent woman so no man could do that to her. And the only way to teach her was to show her."

Finally Alex spoke. "I still don't see what that has to do with you not confiding in me. We're engaged, Amanda. You can't keep secrets from me."

"I didn't feel I was keeping secrets. You and I happened so fast . . . I found myself wanting to please you, sometimes the same way I wanted to please Jeff. And I guess without thinking about it, I didn't want your disapproval. So it seemed safer not to tell you."

"Safer?"

"We're getting married in two weeks, Alex. And we were so happy, I knew you wouldn't want me to see Jeff."

"So this is my fault?"

"I just didn't want to upset you. And once Jeff told

me what he wanted, I knew you wouldn't want me to take the money. But Alex, this is *my* decision to make. Heather is my daughter, and I have to do what is best for her, whether you approve of that or not."

When Alex turned toward her, she could see the anger in the set of his jaw, in the deep green of his eyes. His voice was low but clear as he said, "Not only didn't you trust me enough to confide in me, but you didn't trust me enough to put Heather first. If we marry, I'll make sure she has money for a college education, the same way as I will for Kristy. And you're right—I do want you to refuse the money. I don't want your ex-husband controlling any part of your life. And with what you've told me, there's a good chance he'd want to."

Amanda swallowed hard as her heart raced. She knew she had to say what was on her mind. "Yet you want to control the decisions I make?"

"I don't want to control your decisions, but I want input if I'm going to be your husband. You didn't give me that chance." His tone told her he resented everything about what had happened, and he still felt betrayed. Her throat tightened, and she blinked twice to stem tears that threatened. She wouldn't cry and make him feel sorry for her. The last thing she wanted was his pity.

Drawing on the strength she'd needed after her divorce, she pointed out, "You've used the word if twice now. *Are* we going to get married?"

The water in the creek rushed past rocks and rippled along its banks. "I don't know the answer to that right now. I think we both have heavy thinking to do." This time, a stray cheer from the baseball game and a few birds chirping in the trees above couldn't fill the silence between them.

When Alex broke it, he asked, "Are you going to refuse the money?"

"Is that a condition for us getting married?" The idea that Alex wanted the same kind of control Jeff had wanted made her heart ache.

Alex didn't answer her, but rather stood. "I don't think we have anything else to talk about. I can't understand your point of view, and you can't understand mine. Stalemate. I'll take you home, and then go get the girls. It will be easier if I just drop Heather off."

What he meant was the pain of being together was worse than the pain of being apart. Or maybe he didn't mind being apart. That was the impression he was giving. Maybe he'd only wanted a mother for Kristy and a bed partner, and maybe love hadn't entered into it at all.

That thought made Amanda pull her pride tighter around her. She wouldn't let him see how much she hurt because she wouldn't let him see how much she loved him.

The creek looked more like a small river on Saturday afternoon as Kristy and Heather stood by its bank, tossing stones into the water and watching them swirl away. "What are we gonna do?" Kristy asked.

"Mom was crying last night," Heather said morosely. "She thought I couldn't hear her, but I could."

"Dad was so quiet. He didn't even talk to me at breakfast this morning. It was weird."

"I think they still wanna get married. They just don't know it," Heather decided.

"Do you think if we got them into the same room together it would help?" Kristy wanted to know.

Usually Kristy came up with all the ideas, but this time Heather had one of her own. "I can think of something even better." And she smiled at her friend and started explaining exactly what they were going to do.

The Sunday baseball game on the TV didn't distract Alex as it was intended to. It was almost five o'clock, and he supposed he should be thinking about making the girls something for supper. Kristy had asked him if Heather could come and play for the afternoon and evening. Knowing the girls still felt responsible for what was happening between him and Amanda, he hadn't wanted to keep them apart, so he'd agreed. They'd played up in Kristy's room most of the afternoon, then gone outside. Every once in a while he heard them going in and out of the kitchen, and he wondered what they were doing. But he figured they couldn't get into any trouble in there. And the truth was—every time he looked at Heather, he saw her mother. All he could think about were Amanda's big blue eyes and the taste of her kiss.

Damn, he'd had a narrow escape. They hadn't canceled the wedding yet, but he didn't see how they could go forward with it, either. What kind of marriage could they have if she didn't consult him about major decisions? What kind of marriage could they have if she thought of her daughter as somehow separate from his? What kind of marriage could they have if she went behind his back every time she thought he wouldn't approve of something she wanted to do?

There weren't any answers to those kind of questions. Alex switched off the baseball game and stared at the blank screen, wondering how he could have done this to himself a second time. His world seemed to be in chaos, just as it had been when Rhonda discovered that one impulsive night of lovemaking had caused her pregnancy.

One impulsive night.

Alex swore long and hard. He and Amanda hadn't used protection! They'd thought they were getting married. What if she was already pregnant?

His mind couldn't quite encompass that idea, though it was easy to imagine her expecting his child, glowing with the beauty only pregnant women could have. He could imagine her stroking her tummy, letting him feel the baby move. Damn it, he had to stop this. If she was pregnant . . .

He'd deal with it if it happened.

But as he switched on the baseball game once more, the thought of Amanda carrying his child gave him pleasure and pain until he didn't know which was worse.

Amanda drove home from shopping in Camp Hill, not looking forward to spending Sunday evening alone. After lunch Kristy had called and asked if Heather could come up to play for the afternoon and evening. Amanda had agreed so her daughter would know she wasn't upset with her or Kristy. There was no reason the two girls should be miserable just because their parents were.

But then maybe Alex *wasn't* miserable. She didn't know how he felt; she didn't know what to do.

But she'd messed up everything by trying not to make waves, by trying to avoid Alex's disapproval, by not taking the chance that he loved her. Did he love her? And if he had before, did he still? Or had she ruined everything?

Pulling into her carport, she switched off the engine and felt such loneliness and sadness that she was immobilized for a few moments. But then she sighed and got out, gathered the school supplies she'd bought from the backseat and went around to the back door of the house. She'd left it open so if Heather needed anything, she could get it easily.

Amanda stood inside the kitchen for a moment, packages in hand, listening to the silence. Sighing again, she took the packages to the table and set them down. She supposed she should make herself something for supper, but she wasn't hungry. Maybe she'd make lemonade for later, for when Heather came home. The idea perked her up a little, and she went to the refrigerator to see if she had enough lemons. That's when she saw the note hanging under an apple magnet in the middle of the door.

Dear Mom,

Kristy and I really need to talk to you. Can you meet us at the lean-to at six o'clock?

It's very, very important.

Love,
Heather

Amanda checked her watch. It was five-thirty. She wondered why the girls hadn't just come down here, but then she realized Alex wouldn't let them come to an empty house. And if he called to make sure she was home, he'd have to talk to her. Kristy and Heather probably figured that this was the easiest way under the circumstances. She couldn't help but worry that they were troubled about something. All she could do was try to reassure them that even if she and Alex didn't marry, they wouldn't interfere in the girls' friendship. At least she wouldn't. Would Alex?

Had he already? Is that why they wanted this meeting?

There was no point driving herself crazy. She'd soon find out. Making a quick trip to the bathroom to freshen up, she brushed her hair back into a ponytail. She thought briefly about reapplying lipstick, then shrugged. She wouldn't be seeing Alex. The lean-to was far enough away from the house that he couldn't see what was going on down there.

After she'd changed from her sandals to her sneakers, she walked down her back yard to the property line and then followed it past the other yards that separated her house from Alex's. The ground was uneven along the woods that bordered all the yards. She could hear the creek, its banks full. The birds calling to each other in the early evening, the long shadows, the shaded trees overhead normally would have brought a smile to Amanda's face and given her a sense of peace and well-being. But she could only think about Alex and the wedding that might not take place.

Two bushy-tailed squirrels raced in front of her, chasing each other up a tree. In one of the back yards, Amanda saw three children playing on the swing set, their laughter carrying as far as the woods. She remembered Alex asking her if she wanted more children. She remembered him making love to her—fervently, slowly, sweetly.

Tears threatened again, and she told herself she had to come up with a plan. She had to prove to Alex in some way that she loved him and wanted to spend her life with him. But as the lean-to came into view, her main concern at the moment was comforting Kristy and Heather, trying to assure them that their friendship didn't have to dissolve just because their parents' engagement might.

As she came close to the lean-to, she didn't hear the girls' voices. Maybe they weren't here yet. Checking her watch, she saw that she was five minutes early. But as she walked up to the lean-to and peeked inside, she frowned. The three-sided structure that faced the woods wasn't sheltering two nine-year-old girls, but rather what looked like a picnic. There were two place settings—two dishes, two sets of silverware, two napkins and two glasses. Placed in one corner was a plate of sandwiches wrapped in plastic wrap. An unopened bag of potato chips and a dish of strawberries sat in the other corner. Looking more closely, Amanda saw two candy bars sticking out from under the bag of chips. She didn't know what was going on until she spotted Alex walking toward her, looking none too happy now that he'd spied her.

When he was a few feet away, he said, "I don't know what's going on. I went into the kitchen to start supper and found a note on the refrigerator from Kristy asking me to meet her and Heather down here."

"I came home to a note, too. Heather asked me to be here at six o'clock, but now that I see what's here . . ." She motioned to the inside of the lean-to.

Coming around the corner but making a wide path around her, he looked inside the wooden frame, then ran his hand through his hair. "They set us up again."

"Don't be angry, Alex. They're just trying to—"

"I know what they're trying to do, and I'm not angry. I'm just frustrated. I don't know how to handle Kristy anymore than I know what to do about us."

The drone of an airplane overhead was the only sound for a few moments.

If only she and Alex could start really talking, if only he could understand. Maybe even just a short time alone together could help. "They've gone to a lot of trouble."

"You want us to sit down and have a picnic and pretend nothing happened?"

She shook her head. "No, of course not. But maybe their idea isn't so farfetched. Maybe if we just took some deep breaths and sat down and had the picnic . . ."

He looked at her as if she were reaching for the moon.

"Alex, they think everything is their fault. Maybe we should at least try to show them it isn't."

Searching her face as if trying to find the woman he once cared about, he finally said, "All right. They're probably up in Kristy's room with a pair of binoculars watching us."

"At least they can't see us if we're sitting inside," she responded, hoping the privacy of the small space might bring them closer together. But when they ducked under the low roof and sat on the blanket that the girls had folded there, their knees almost touched and the tension between them was even worse than when they'd been standing outside.

Peeking out from behind the cover of trees, Kristy and Heather watched Alex and Amanda intently. "I can't hear what they're saying," Kristy complained.

Heather came out from behind the tree to try to see better. "They're sitting inside. At least Mom didn't go back to the house. But I can't see them now."

Knowing her dad and Amanda couldn't see her from within the lean-to, Kristy stepped away from her tree, too. "Let's go climb to our lookout. We can't hear or see here. Maybe up there we can see something."

Heather nodded her agreement.

They didn't have to go very far until they stood at the bank before the log that crossed the creek. Today, with the water high, swirls of waves almost touched the fallen tree whose bark was still wet and soaked from showers last night.

Heather had never liked crossing the makeshift bridge. She was sure the last few times she had, it had creaked and wobbled more. And today the foaming water as it swept along its path bothered her more than usual. "Do you really think we should do this?"

Kristy took a step up onto the fallen tree and balanced herself. "Sure, we've done it a hundred times before. C'mon, we'll be fine."

But Heather wasn't so sure as she followed behind her friend, imitating a high-wire act.

Ten

Amanda felt Alex's gaze on her as she took a bite of one of the ham and cheese sandwiches the girls had made. She thought maybe if they talked about a safe subject they could get back on a less tense footing, but she wasn't sure what a safe subject was. "At least when school starts, you'll know that Kristy isn't going to really have problems with math."

Alex picked up half of a sandwich from the plate. "Right."

If she was going to be the only one talking, this was going to be a quiet meal. "Alex, we don't have to go through this charade if it's going to be too much trouble for you."

"It's not too much trouble. It's just difficult."

"And you don't think it's difficult for me, too? That I don't want to know what's going to happen next, or what we should do about the girls? Or if you're ever going to look at me again as if you care?" She wouldn't let him see her cry; she absolutely wouldn't. Her pride was the only thing she had left.

At least he looked a bit chagrined. "All right. Let's take the question with the highest priority. What are we going to do about the girls?"

"All we can do is reassure them they can still be

friends no matter what happens with us. I won't keep Heather from seeing Kristy."

"And I won't keep Kristy from seeing Heather," he agreed matter-of-factly.

"They think our problems are their fault."

"We'll just have to keep telling them they're wrong. In time—"

"What's time going to do, Alex? Do we just let time pass until there is no wedding? Should I tell the real estate agent not to list the house on Monday? Will time help you realize that I did what I thought was best?"

The space inside the lean-to reverberated with her question, and they gazed at each other looking for answers, looking for the future.

"Do you still think you did what was best?" Alex asked in a low voice.

It was so hard for her to speak past the lump in her throat. They were on the verge of really talking, and if she could just make him understand—

"Mom! Mom!" The scream carried to the lean-to, and Amanda immediately knew it belonged to her daughter.

She scrambled outside, and jumped to her feet, calling, "Heather, where are you?" Her daughter's voice had seemed to come at her from four different directions, and she couldn't get her bearings. Alex had said the girls were in Kristy's room, but as she turned toward the house, she heard again, "Mom, at the creek. Hurry!"

Amanda took off at a run, not knowing if Alex was behind her or not. All she cared about was getting to her daughter. Heather wouldn't have yelled like that unless . . . "Heather!" she called into the woods.

"Mom! Here!" her daughter screamed back, her voice breaking.

It only took moments to spot her, but it seemed like much longer. In a glance, Amanda guessed what had happened. A narrow tree trunk that the girls had apparently been using as a bridge across the creek had broken in two. Heather was knee deep in water, hanging on to a tree limb that draped over the bank. But the bank was muddy, and she couldn't seem to get her footing to crawl up.

As soon as Heather saw Amanda, she pointed to the middle of the creek. Kristy had fallen into the deepest part. She was holding onto the broken trunk, but all of her was submerged except for her head and arm.

Dear God, let her be all right, Amanda prayed. Seeing Heather was in no immediate danger, she half-slid, half-crawled down the side of the muddy creek bank into the swirling water. She heard Alex call, "Amanda, wait!"

But she couldn't wait. If Kristy let go, the water could sweep her farther down, and she could get hurt even more than she might be already. Without a thought for her own safety, Amanda waded through the mud until her feet didn't touch. Then she swam to Kristy, praying all the way. When she reached Alex's daughter, she saw how pale she was . . . and scared.

Curling her arm around the little girl's waist, Amanda asked, "Are you hurt? Can you tell?"

Kristy shook her head. "I—I don't think so. I felt it breaking and sorta jumped. I can move my legs and everything. I just got so scared, I was afraid to let go."

"It's okay. I'm here now. You can let go. I'll keep my arm around you, and we'll swim toward the bank together. Okay?"

It was a good thirty feet to the bank, and Amanda could tell Kristy didn't want to release her hold on the log. She looked into Amanda's eyes for reassurance.

"We can do this, honey. Come on."

It was the encouragement the nine-year-old needed. She let go of the trunk, and Amanda started swimming. As soon as her feet touched the creek bed, she clasped Kristy close to her, almost carrying her in the water until Alex met them and took his daughter from her. He'd already helped Heather to the safety of solid ground above the creek bank. When he reached the edge of the water, he climbed out and set Kristy down. Then he rushed back to Amanda and held out his hand to her. She took it and managed to scramble up the bank. Heather and Kristy hugged her. As Amanda held both of them close protectively, she didn't let go.

Tears stung Alex's eyes as he watched Kristy and Heather huddled close to Amanda. He didn't think he could love Amanda any more than he loved her at this moment. And the startling realization of that love rocked him. When he'd asked her to marry him, he'd thought it would be the expedient thing to do. Both of their daughters needed two parents. The chemistry between them was explosive enough to make every night of their marriage a night of pleasure. The thought of romantic love had never even entered his mind, probably because he'd almost forgotten what the concept meant. Years ago he had fallen in love and had been rewarded with terrible disappointment and disillusionment. Oh, he knew he loved his daughter, but he'd thought that was the only kind of love he'd ever feel again.

He'd been so wrong.

What was even more wrong was that he'd never told

Amanda exactly how much he cared about her, how much he loved her. No wonder she hadn't been able to confide in him! No wonder she'd been afraid of his disapproval. He'd been a jerk, and since their argument he'd treated her so badly.

Could she forgive him?

She had risked her own safety for his daughter. He'd never met a woman who was that unselfish, that giving. And if he had the chance, he'd prove to her that no problem was ever too big to solve, and any disagreement could be resolved if they talked and compromised.

If only he could have seen this clearly before.

Breathing around a painful tightness in his chest, he moved closer to the two girls and the woman he loved. "Are you all right?" he asked, not sure who to address first.

Heather slid from her mother's embrace. "I'm fine. Just wet and muddy."

Kristy looked up at him. "I think I'm okay."

Taking her by the shoulders, he examined her from head to toe. Her one leg was scraped, and she was covered with splotches of mud. But other than that, she looked amazingly okay, except for the goose bumps on her arms.

"Let's get you out of those wet clothes, and put some antibiotic cream on your leg. After you're cleaned up and dry, I'll give you the scolding you deserve."

Kristy's eyes grew wide with apology. "Dad, I'm sorry. We just wanted to see what was going on."

"How many times did you cross the creek over that trunk this summer?"

"About a hundred," she murmured.

Then he looked at Heather. "One of you should

have known better, but we'll talk about that later. Come on, let's get you up to the house."

He hadn't met Amanda's gaze yet. He didn't know how to tell her that he thought she was the bravest woman alive, that he loved her so much he never wanted to let her out of his sight. But she was shivering, too, and he didn't want to rush what he had to say to her.

"I'd go to my house," she started, "but I don't think my legs will take me that far."

He wanted to swing her up into his arms and carry her like he had that day in the cave. But he wasn't sure she'd let him or how she'd react, as independent as she was. "I have lots of spare shirts that'll fit you just fine," he said.

Her eyes were wide, and he didn't know if he saw sadness there or regret. But whatever she was feeling, she nodded and took the girls' hands.

While Amanda and the girls cleaned up in the large upstairs bathroom, Alex showered in the smaller bathroom next to his bedroom. As he dressed, he thought about what he wanted to say to Amanda, but nothing seemed right. Taking a white shirt from his closet, he went down the hall and knocked on Kristy's bedroom door. Knowing the girls needed their privacy and Amanda would probably want hers, he said, "Amanda, I hung my shirt on the doorknob. I'll be downstairs."

He hoped that was enough of an invitation for her to come down, but if it wasn't, he'd be back up here in a heartbeat.

Downstairs, he paced, wishing he had enough time to go buy her some flowers, or a pearl necklace, or something. But then he remembered the daylilies blooming at the side of the house. It would only take him a minute to collect some of them.

He was just re-entering the living room when he saw her coming down the stairs. She looked self-conscious in his shirt, even though it practically went to her knees. Her feet were bare, and she must have dried her hair with Kristy's dryer because it was soft and wavy around her face. She looked so beautiful, and he didn't know where to start.

When she saw the flowers in his hand, she tilted her head and looked surprised. "They're pretty."

Crossing to her, he held them out. "They're for you. They should be diamonds, or emeralds, or something worth a whole lot more because you risked your life to save my daughter's."

The hope in her eyes faded as she took them. "She was in trouble. I helped her. That's all. The same way you helped Heather." After a deep breath, she rushed on, "Alex, I have to tell you something, and if I don't tell you now, I might not have the courage to later. I love you. I never said it because I guess I was afraid to, just as I was afraid to trust in you enough to confide in you about Jeff. I'm sorry I didn't tell you. I never want to keep anything from you. I guess I'm trying to ask you if you can possibly forgive me—"

Pressing his fingers to her lips, he said, "I'm sorry I reacted so strongly. I haven't fought my desire for you, Amanda. But I have fought all the feelings, so I never told you what they were. You didn't trust me because you didn't know how very much I love you."

At her small gasp, he took her in his arms, flowers and all. "Can you forgive me?" Feeling her shoulders start to shake, he realized she was crying. Pulling back, he watched the tears as they streamed down her cheeks, and he swallowed hard. "It doesn't matter what decision you make about Heather's college fund. I'll love you no matter what, through everything. Or is it too late? Have I ruined our chances?"

But when she shook her head and tried to give him a small smile, he suspected reaction was setting in from everything that had happened. This time he didn't think she'd care if he swung her into his arms and carried her to the sofa. So he did, and she hung on as if he were her lifeline.

Sitting down with her, he held her close. "When I saw you go into that creek after Kristy—" He stopped, emotion clogging his throat. But at Amanda's understanding expression, he continued. "We protected each other's children, Amanda, without a second thought, and I think we do trust each other. We just need to build on that trust."

"But can you forgive me?" she asked.

Stroking her tears from her cheek, he said, "Yes, I can forgive you. Can you forgive my insufferable righteousness? I love you, Amanda. I want to spend my life with you. Will you still marry me?"

Wrapping her arms around his neck, she smiled. "Yes, I'll marry you."

When he bent his head, and his lips met hers, her kiss told him she forgave him as well, and she wanted a future with him as much as he wanted a future with her.

At the top of the stairs, Kristy and Heather gave each other high-fives and smiled broadly.

The sky was cloudless, a beautiful shade of blue. Approximately fifty people—friends, acquaintances, neighbors and relatives—sat in the rows of white chairs facing the flower-covered trellis where the minister stood. Amanda's heart overflowed with happiness and her pulse beat rapidly with the excitement of the day as the music from violins filled Alex's back yard. Kristy started down the white runner toward the trellis.

In front of her, dressed in the same pink taffeta as her best friend, Heather glanced over her shoulder. "Are you ready, Mom?"

Not an hour before when Alex's mom had helped her into the cream lace wedding dress, Amanda knew she'd never been more ready. As she'd clasped around her neck the string of pearls that Alex had given her last night, she'd remembered his tender kiss and the promise of the future that had glowed in his eyes. "I'm ready, honey."

Heather gave her one last smile, then started forward.

The daylilies in her bridal bouquet trembled in her hand as Amanda took a deep breath, then set her gaze on the man she was about to marry.

Alex was standing with the minister, watching Kristy and then Heather walk down the aisle. But when Heather reached the front row of chairs, his gaze found Amanda's. She started walking forward and didn't stop until he took her hand in his, clasping it with the strength and protectiveness that she knew would wrap around her and the girls for the rest of their lives.

Amanda handed her bouquet to Alex's mother who was seated in the front row. Then with Kristy at Alex's side and Heather at hers, she faced forward with him.

The minister welcomed the guests, then said a few

words about marriage and why they were gathered there. And when it came time for their vows, Alex and Amanda faced each other and held hands.

At the minister's nod, Alex began, his face more serious than Amanda had ever seen it. "I, Alex, take you, Amanda, for a life of love, sharing and caring. I promise I will do my best to respect you always, to listen to you, and to understand you. No matter what our road together brings, I will stand beside you as a partner, support you, and give you anything you need and everything I have to give. If we disagree, I promise to see your point of view and to talk and share with you until we find a solution to any problem we have. I will cherish you for the rest of our lives."

When they had decided to write their own vows, they'd also decided not to share them until their wedding day. Amanda's eyes filled with tears at Alex's words, and she knew he meant every one of them. She could hardly speak as she saw the world of love he wanted to give her in his eyes.

But somehow she managed to remember the words she'd written down and memorized in the past few days. "I, Amanda, take you, Alex, to be my husband and life partner. I promise to love you and honor you and respect you for all of our days. I promise to laugh with you and play with you and love you, telling you my feelings so you don't have to guess and helping you talk about yours. I will spend each day thinking about your happiness as well as mine and will do everything in my power to meet your needs. As we grow old together, I will not let the sun set on hurt or anger and will keep my heart open to everything you have to say. I vow to love you through light and dark and to be the best wife I know how to be."

Alex's eyes filled with emotion at her words and he squeezed her hand. When he slid the wedding band onto Amanda's finger, a tear escaped down her cheek. With a tender smile, he wiped it away with his thumb. After she slid a band of gold onto his finger, he whispered, "I love you."

Then, secure in each others' hearts, they added something special to the ceremony. Alex took Heather's hand, and Amanda took Kristy's. Then the four of them made a circle.

The minister beamed down at them, blessed them and said, "I now pronounce Alex and Amanda man and wife, and I pronounce Alex, Amanda, Heather and Kristy a family."

The four of them hugged, and then Kristy, Heather and all the guests watched as Alex and Amanda sealed the ceremony and their lives together with a kiss.

Epilogue

Twenty-one months later

Alex took the statement that had come in the mail up to the bedroom. Amanda had gotten home later than he had tonight, after a faculty meeting at school. She'd given him a terrific hello kiss that was still thrumming through him and told him she was going to get a shower. It wasn't until he'd opened the mail and saw the mutual fund statement that he'd decided he'd take it upstairs for Amanda to see. On the way up, he remembered the girls would be at softball practice for another hour yet. He and Amanda could enjoy a pleasurable two-for-one shower and have some fun at the same time. They'd be married two years come August—the happiest, most fulfilling two years of his entire life.

When he entered the bedroom, Amanda was coming out of the bathroom. She hadn't showered yet—she was still wearing the pretty blue linen dress she'd worn to school that day. She smiled at him and there was something so tender in her smile . . .

Crossing to her, he handed her the statement he'd brought upstairs. "Heather's college fund is really growing. You made a wise decision accepting Jeff's offer."

"*We* made the right decision in accepting Jeff's offer."

Since they'd married, they made all their decisions together for both the girls. When Amanda had let Jeff know she and Alex would agree to the college fund, her ex-husband had asked if he could write to Heather. Knowing it would mean a lot to him, realizing he was trying to change his life on many levels, Amanda had discussed that with Alex, too. They'd agreed that it was a good idea for Heather to stay in contact with her father.

Jeff didn't write often, but when he did, Heather was glad to get his letters, and she eagerly wrote back. But she had started calling Alex "Dad" soon after the wedding, and he was the one who cheered her on at softball games, taught her how to play tennis, and hugged her whenever she needed it. Kristy had begun calling Amanda "Mom" at the same time, and Alex suspected that the girls had arranged that as well.

Taking Amanda in his arms, Alex kissed her temple and murmured, "I'll have to add to Kristy's account so she can keep up."

Amanda pulled away slightly and looked up at him.

"Is something wrong?" he asked.

Her eyes were very bright, and he could see uncertainty in them and wondered why.

"No. Nothing's wrong. It's just—" She stopped for a moment, then went on. "We need to open another account, another college account."

Why would they need to open another college account? Unless . . .

Her smile was radiant as she lifted up a small plastic stick she held in her hand. "I got a plus sign. That means we're going to have a baby."

They'd decided to let nature take its course and just enjoy the family they had while they hoped for a child together. Now their hopes had been realized. Wrapping his arms around Amanda's waist, he swung her up and twirled them in a circle. "Pregnant! We're pregnant!"

Laughing, she rested her hands on his shoulders and looked down at him with love. "I guess you're happy about this?"

"Ecstatic. How about you?"

"Ecstatic."

Then Alex lowered her slowly until he captured her lips and kissed her with all the passion and promise he'd offered her on their wedding day. He was so grateful to her for giving him the chance to love so wondrously, so completely.

Amanda's response told him she was not only grateful, too, but supremely happy.

And as they undressed each other and made love slowly with renewed commitment, their hearts rejoiced that they'd found each other, and their souls joined in a union as precious as the new life Amanda carried. They were partners for a lifetime.

Partners in love.

Partners forever.

A perfect match.

ABOUT THE AUTHOR

Karen Rose Smith began reading romances as a teenager. Formerly an English teacher and home decorator, when back surgery interrupted her lifestyle, she began writing them! Happily married for twenty-seven years, she believes everyone needs hope in an ideal and an escape from time to time. And that's why she can see herself writing romance novels for a long time to come. Ms. Smith enjoys hearing from her readers. They can write to her at P.O. Box 1545, Hanover, PA 17331.